TED AND TERRI
and the
BROKEN ARROW

TED AND TERRI
and the
BROKEN ARROW

by
BERNARD PALMER

MOODY PRESS
CHICAGO

© 1971 by
THE MOODY BIBLE INSTITUTE
OF CHICAGO

Printed in the United States of America

Contents

Chapter		Page
1	An Alarming Discovery	7
2	An Embarrassing Predicament	14
3	Be Careful, Terri!	24
4	A Vicious Companion	33
5	A Broken Friendship	42
6	A New Plan of Action	48
7	New Problems	58
8	A New Threat	67
9	New Arrivals	76
10	The Obnoxious Apes	85
11	One Nice Ape	95
12	An Unexpected Foe	105
13	Safe at Last	117

1

An Alarming Discovery

The late afternoon sun slid silently through the pale Colorado skies until it perched beyond the distant peaks, a golden halo about the rocky pinnacle. Although it was almost gone, a few scattered rays still slanted through the trees, lengthening the shadows across the tortuous mountain trail. The day had been warm when Ted Walker and Pete Ellison left the horse barn of the M-Bar-H Dude Ranch and rode up the steep mountainside. But now that the sun was about to set, it seemed to have lost its warmth; and the freshening breeze put a chill in the air.

Ted and his twin sister, Terri, had only been at the dude ranch a couple of days, and it didn't seem possible that they were actually going to spend the whole summer there. Resting his hands on the saddle horn, Ted turned to his companion.

"I'm sure glad that your dad thought of us when

he took over the M-Bar-H and realized that you were going to need help for the summer."

"So am I." Pete smiled.

They rode on for a moment or two in comparative silence.

"Terri and I had such a great time when we were here a year ago that we made up our minds right away, as soon as we got your letter."

Pete chuckled. "You two were the first ones we contacted when we started to get a summer crew together." He didn't tell Ted that he had been the one to suggest the twins even before his dad bought the dude ranch and began to plan for the summer season. He didn't have to. Ted had a good idea that his friend had been responsible, at least partially, for their being invited to work on the ranch that summer.

Ted reined in for a moment and, standing in the stirrups, looked down the steep pine-covered slope and across the lush valley. There was something about the Rockies that stilled his voice and made him feel closer than ever to God. For a moment his very being was enveloped by the beauty around him, and he felt as though God was actually standing at his side. It was a strange, reverent feeling that he hadn't experienced since they left the mountains the summer before.

"It's sure going to be great to have you and Terri

An Alarming Discovery

working with us this summer," Pete said, breaking the mood of the moment.

His companion nodded. "You can say that again. At least it's going to be great for us. When we got your letter, we could hardly believe that it was true; and when Mother and Dad said we could come, we were sure that we must have been dreaming."

They started to ride forward once more, slowly, the well-trained horses picking their way with care.

"Terri ought to be happy, too, now that Sam Hall and Gary Bordon are back."

Ted glanced quickly at his friend. "How come your dad hired those two weirdos back this summer?"

Pete's grin showed that he agreed with Ted's appraisal of the other two workers. "That's something that I've been wondering myself. They're sure not that good when it comes to working."

"I haven't seen them do anything except flirt with Terri, and she's stupid enough to love it."

The corners of Pete's mouth twitched. "To tell you the truth, I believe the former owner had something to do with it. One of those characters is a relative of his. I think that's the reason Dad decided to use them."

"I figured it would have to be something like that. It's a cinch that he didn't rehire them because of the amount of work they did last summer."

They rode on for several minutes without saying anything more. Ted was thinking about his sister again when he caught a flash of tan in the brush ahead of them. He reined in suddenly.

"Did you see that?" Ted asked with surprise.

"See what?"

"I thought sure I spotted Prince Atlas just ahead of us." His voice was hushed.

Pete shook his head. "I don't think so. Somebody was telling me the other day that he saw tracks around the old sheepherder's cabin where we kept him last year. I figured that would have to be Prince."

Ted thought about that. It seemed unlikely that the young elk would stay around the old buildings as long as that. After all, he hadn't been penned there more than a few months and had been free almost a year. "Do you really think he would do that?" he asked. "I mean, do you think he would stay around those buildings for so long?"

Pete shrugged. "I've seen him in that same general area a few times, so I guess I just figured he was the one who was making those tracks."

Ted wiped the sweat from his forehead with the back of his hand. "You may be right." He stood up in the saddle and looked around. "I sure thought about him a lot during the hunting season last fall when I kept reading about all the elk that were

An Alarming Discovery

being killed here in Colorado. A couple of times I was going to write and ask you if he'd been shot."

"You aren't the only one who's been concerned about him," Pete continued. "To tell you the truth, I wouldn't have been surprised at all if he had been killed. He's so tame I can still get within a dozen feet of him." A smile caught the corners of his mouth. "You know, I think he still remembers me. He'll start to come up to me, but he won't quite do it. He acts like he remembers me but can't quite make up his mind whether I'll hurt him or not."

Ted took hold of the saddle horn briefly as the trail steepened. "I'm sure anxious to see him and find out how he's doing."

It was a ride of over an hour up to the old sheepherder's place. They followed the steep, twisting trail over one ridge, into a narrow valley, and up Bald Mountain to the place where Pete had first kept Prince Atlas penned. The nearer they got to the ramshackle buildings, the quieter the two boys became. Their eyes narrowed as they searched the area ahead for a glimpse of the young bull elk.

"How about it? Do you usually see him when you come up here?"

Pete frowned. Actually, it had been two or three months since he had seen the elk that used to be his pet. "No, I don't always see Prince every time I come up to the old shack, so it wouldn't necessarily mean anything if we didn't see him this afternoon. But it wouldn't necessarily mean that he was all right, either."

They rode up to the old shack in silence and dismounted. Ted was still looking nervously in every direction, his gaze searching the brush that ringed the little clearing, as though fearful of what they would find.

"I'm beginning to wonder if he's around here this afternoon."

"Me, too."

They dropped the reins so their mounts would stand still, and they began to walk around looking for some sign that would indicate the young bull elk had been there recently. Ted shuffled through the parched grass, looking for tracks, although he knew there would be little chance of seeing any tracks in the hard ground. He had almost reached the cabin when he kicked something with his foot. He paused and stooped to pick it up.

"Hey, what's this?" He showed Pete the broken arrow he held in his hand.

Pete grinned. "We'd better dash for the fort—the Indians are coming!"

"If you ask me, I'd say they're already here." Ted turned the length of arrow slowly between his fingers.

"It looks to me as if somebody came up here to

An Alarming Discovery

do some target shooting, but I can't figure out why anyone would want to come so far, just for that."

Pete's eyes narrowed, and he ran a finger gingerly along the razor-edge of the arrowhead. "This isn't a target arrow, Ted. Whoever shot this arrow was hunting!"

Ted stiffened. That *was* a hunting arrow. And it hadn't been lying on the ground more than a day or two; there wasn't any rust on the head. "Do you have a bow-and-arrow season here?"

"We do in the fall, but this arrow wasn't broken that long ago."

Ted was staring at the bush beyond the clearing. Could someone have been shooting at Prince Atlas? Was that the reason he and Pete hadn't seen the young bull? The very thought chilled him!

2

An Embarrassing Predicament

Terri Walker's hours were different at the M-Bar-H than those of Pete and her brother, Ted. She was always busy waiting tables at mealtime, and once in a while she was expected to be available for babysitting in the afternoon or evening.

Ted didn't think she would be able to date as much as she wanted to, and he teased her about it; but she still had plenty of time for the boys. Occasionally she went riding with a young guest who had been properly introduced, and of course Gary and Sam were always there. She liked them both and dated them indiscriminately, going with whichever one asked her first.

There were other fellows in both Harper and Cotesville whom she would have enjoyed dating more than either Gary or Sam, but she was far away from Michigan. She had to admit that they both treated her with consideration and respect.

An Embarrassing Predicament

They were gentlemen when they were with her and dating them did give her something to do.

She knew that Ted didn't think much of either of the fellows they worked with, but she couldn't let that bother her. She couldn't figure out why, but he didn't seem to like any of the fellows she chose to date.

Gary and Sam took her out regularly, competing with each other to find interesting things to do. On one date she would be taken horseback riding on beautiful mountain trails. On the next they would go fishing, or have a picnic beside a swift-moving stream. Occasionally she would suggest that they walk along one of the nearby trails, enjoying the quiet of the evening and the play of color on the distant slopes as the sun made ready to slip away for the night. All in all, it started out as an enjoyable summer for Terri.

Gary was the first one to suggest that they leave the ranch for a date. "There's something I just learned yesterday," he said one late afternoon, as they sat around their little picnic fire after barbecuing hamburgers. "Did you know there's a little nightclub between here and town?"

She eyed him warily. Up until then she had managed to steer the conversation away from such things. "I have heard something about it. It's called the Eagle's Nest, isn't it?"

"I think that's the name. Anyway, there's a new singing group appearing there next week. Harry's Apes!"

In spite of herself, she was interested. She had heard a lot about the group. They were supposed to be the hottest thing on the music scene since the Beatles came over from Liverpool. They packed out the places where they appeared and had made three million-dollar records. Excitement gleamed in her eyes.

"You've got to be kidding. A group as popular as they are wouldn't come to a little place like this."

"It may seem like a little place to you, but the way I get it, it's not. They say it's one of the best and most popular nightclubs in this part of Colorado. They have all the top entertainers here at some time or other, and they get reservations from people who live as far away as Denver. It's a plush club."

She hesitated, anticipating where his conversation was leading and wishing that she had some way of stopping him without embarrassing both of them.

"I'd sure like to hear Harry's Apes sometime, wouldn't you?" Gary's voice rose apprehensively.

"It would be all right, I guess." She tried not to sound particularly interested. "I've got a couple of

An Embarrassing Predicament

their records. I bought them in Denver on the way out here."

"Seeing them in person and hearing them would be a lot more exciting than having some records. How about it? Wouldn't you like to go with me?"

She gave him a sidelong look. She knew well enough what her folks would think if she went to a place like the Eagle's Nest and they found out about it. She knew how uneasy she felt just thinking about how nice it would be to go and hear them. That nagging conscience of hers began to prod her. Now she would have to tell him why it was that she could not go there with him. That wouldn't be so bad if she could do it without getting him to think so terribly of her. Gary had already dropped enough hints to let her know what he thought of people who, as he called it, went "overboard on religion." She couldn't have him laugh at her and call her a square. And she would just die if he spread the story around the ranch so everybody would know.

"How about it?" he repeated.

"We couldn't go," she protested. "I have to work evenings."

"You can get someone to exchange nights with you. That'll be easy."

She squirmed uncomfortably. She hadn't expected him to come up with that. "But we're under age. We'd get into all kinds of trouble if we go to a place like that where they serve liquor."

He lowered his voice confidently. "This is one of the beautiful things about having the right friends. You see, yesterday I did a favor for the guy who runs the Eagle's Nest. He not only said that he would get you and me in, he's going to give us two of the biggest steaks on the menu. Everthing's free! It's all on the house."

She pulled in a deep breath. This was getting worse. "But we still can get caught," she hedged, "and if that would happen, Mr. Ellison would be furious. He would probably fire both of us."

"Mr. Ellison's not going to know a thing about it and neither's anyone else. Don't get shook. We're not going to get caught."

"We could, easy enough. Then our names would be in the paper and everything."

"You really don't think the sheriff's going to come all the way out from town just to look over the Eagle's Nest, do you?"

She did not answer him.

"Do you know what T. J. told me?" he continued, excitement still glinting in his eyes. "He said that he's expecting that half his business this week will come from the kids around here. They're going to be coming out from town by the carload. It

An Embarrassing Predicament

isn't every day that there's a chance to hear a group like Harry's Apes!"

Going to hear the Apes was tempting, Terri admitted. It would be a blast. Most kids would be so thrilled at the opportunity of going that they wouldn't be able to sleep for a week. But as badly as she wanted to, she knew she couldn't go to a place like the Eagle's Nest. It was against everything she had ever been taught.

It wasn't that she could see anything really wrong with going there. After all, she and Gary would be going just to hear the music. They wouldn't be dancing and they certainly wouldn't be drinking. That was one thing she knew for sure about Gary. He didn't drink. More than once he had told her that he was very much against any kind of liquor.

"Well, how about it?" he demanded, breaking in on her thoughts. "Are you going with me or aren't you?"

The more Terri thought about it the more certain she was that she wanted to go, but still she hesitated. It ought to be enough that she couldn't see anything wrong with going, but it wasn't. She would have to keep it from Ted too. He was as narrow as their folks were when it came to things like that. He would raise a terrible fuss.

"You could take your albums along and get them autographed," he reminded her.

"I—I don't know," she said with growing uneasiness. "I don't know whether I'll be able to make it or not."

Gary flipped his wadded napkin into the smoldering fire. His irritation was apparent. "If *you* don't know whether you'll be able to go, who does?"

Terri moistened her lips with the tip of her tongue. She ought to tell him the real reason why she didn't want to go to the nightclub with him. At least, then he would be able to understand. But she couldn't do that. She couldn't tell Gary and ruin all the good times she was having at the ranch.

"I'll still have to think about it," she told him lamely.

"OK," he said, his expression changing slightly. "You think about it. I'll talk with you tomorrow afternoon. OK?"

"That would be better," she said, nodding gratefully.

"And while you're thinking about it, don't forget that you'll be missing a neat evening if you don't go with me. I'll just have to ask someone else, that's all."

That night, sleep was slow and far away for Terri. Every time she closed her eyes, she saw the brilliant neon sign of the Eagle's Nest, beckoning her to come in.

An Embarrassing Predicament

The more she thought about it the more positive she was that there would be nothing wrong with her going to the nightclub to listen to the music. *Actually, it wouldn't be any different than listening to the music on a stereo or on radio or television,* she reasoned. She wasn't going to make a practice of going to a place where people danced and got drunk and the air was thick with smoke. Actually, aside from hearing the Apes, she had no desire to go there.

The singing group would be appearing at the Eagle's Nest for a few days and would be moving on. She and Gary would go and hear them, and that would be the end of it. When she looked at it that way, she couldn't see that any possible harm could come from her going there for dinner on one particular evening.

Still, her doubts persisted. She didn't know what to do.

On some things she could get Ted's advice, but she didn't dare talk with him about this matter. She already knew what he would say. That made it worse than ever.

The following day when Gary came to the door she was still as far from knowing what she wanted to do as when he first asked her the night before.

"Terri," he said softly, "I hate to bother you while you're working, but I've got to talk with you."

She glanced over her shoulder, half afraid that Mr. or Mrs. Ellison would see her talking with Gary when she was supposed to be working. She didn't dare have that happen. They had always been good to her, but she was very careful to be sure that she gave them a full day's work for her pay.

"You shouldn't have come here," she said, scolding. "I've got work to do. You'll have to see me when I get off after lunch."

"I just wanted to find out if you've made up your mind yet."

She shook her head, dismissing him firmly. "I can't talk now. I'll see you at three o'clock."

She approached three o'clock with foreboding. In a way she hoped that he wouldn't come around. In another way she hoped that he would so she could get it over with.

At three o'clock Gary was waiting to talk with her. She couldn't look at his face because she was still undecided.

"Well, how about it? Are you going with me or aren't you?" he demanded.

She hesitated, drawing in a deep breath.

"I've got to work too, you know." His temper was rising.

Ted was standing in the barn door watching them. She glanced at him helplessly, wishing he would come over and interrupt them.

An Embarrassing Predicament

"If you don't go with me, Terri, I'm going to ask someone else. I want you to know that. This is one evening I'm not passing up for you or anybody."

That did it. Her gaze met his. "All right," she said, defiantly, making up her mind. "I'll go with you!"

3

Be Careful, Terri!

Terri's conscience bothered her repeatedly as she continued to work that evening. She had promised to go to the Eagle's Nest with Gary, reasoning that she could see no harm in it. Now, however, she wondered if she had made the right decision. Her folks usually had good reasons for the things they forbade them to do. She knew that they weren't thinking of their own image in the community. They cared what people thought of them, of course, but not that much. They were thinking about her and Ted. That was what made a decision like this so difficult.

On the other hand she ought to know what would hurt her and what wouldn't. She had to start making her own decisions some time, and she had to have reasons for not going places she wanted to go. She was still thinking about what she had promised Gary when Sam came to go for a walk with her.

Be Careful, Terri! 25

There was something disturbing him. She could see that as soon as he approached. His emotions were always written on his face. When he was sad or happy everybody knew it. Terri said nothing to him about it, but she half suspected that he had been talking with his friend. It didn't take long to find out what was wrong. They hadn't walked more than fifty yards when Sam stopped and pivoted to face her.

"Is it true that you're going to the Eagle's Nest with Gary next week?"

She blushed guiltily. "And what makes you ask that?"

"Is it true, or isn't it?"

She thought she detected a trace of jealousy in his voice. With a mocking smile, she asked, "And what makes you think that I have to answer to you for the things I do or don't do?"

"Is it true, or isn't it?" he repeated.

"I don't think that's any concern of yours."

"You wouldn't go to a place like that with *me*."

Terri folded her arms defensively. "I really can't see that it's any of your business whether I go to the Eagle's Nest or any place else with Gary."

"I guess it really isn't any of my business, Terri," he said, "but I thought you'd go there with *me* to hear the Apes. I've really been counting on it!"

There was a brief hesitation; then a sigh of relief

softened her voice. "You didn't have any reason to count on it until you'd asked me, did you?"

"I suppose not."

"Then that settles it."

Sam groaned aloud. "That's just my luck. I don't know why I didn't get over here to see you before Gary did. I was the one who heard that Harry's Apes were going to be at the Eagle's Nest and told him about it. And then he beat me over here." He shook his head in disgust.

"Maybe you'll have to ask me a little quicker the next time."

Terri's conscience began to twinge again as she got ready for bed that night. She picked up her Bible and opened it for her quiet time. She knew she shouldn't have told Gary that she would go to the nightclub with him. Now that she had already committed herself, the remorse came rushing at her.

Even though she was only going to listen to the music, she still knew it wasn't right. Her folks thought that places like the Eagle's Nest were not suitable places for a Christian to go. They ought to know more about it than she did.

After thinking it over, Terri decided that she wouldn't have agreed to go if she thought that Gary would have understood her reason for not going. But he wouldn't. She was well aware of that. She had tried to talk with him about spiritual things

Be Careful, Terri! 27

before, and he hadn't understood or even tried to.

A tear rolled down her cheek. No matter what she did, things always turned out wrong. She almost decided that there wasn't any use in her even trying to live a Christian life anymore.

She switched out the light and got into bed. As she thought about her problem, a few more tears came. If only there were some Christian fellows around the M-Bar-H for her to date—guys who had the same Christian standards she had—it would be easy for her to live the way she should.

But there weren't any Christian fellows in Cotesville, let alone up on the ranch in the mountains. No one except Pete, and he was too much like a big brother to be interesting to date. He probably didn't care anything about going with girls anyway. He was too busy with horseback riding and working around the ranch. If she didn't go out with guys like Sam and Gary, she would just sit around and vegetate! Nobody could expect her to do *that*.

She began to sob out loud, until she could be heard at the far end of the hall upstairs. She was so miserable she didn't realize that anyone else could hear her.

Ted and Pete were up late that evening, sitting in Pete's room looking over his fishing tackle. The next time they could get away for a few hours they planned on going up to a nearby trout stream to try their luck. Pete was showing Ted his new fly rod when the first faint sound of Terri's sobbing drifted in.

He straightened and looked at Ted quizzically. "What on earth is that?"

Ted frowned to show his disgust. "That," he replied, "is just Terri's way of letting us know that she's still around."

Pete was disturbed by it. "Do you suppose I ought to get Mom to go in and talk to her? Maybe she's sick or something."

"She pulls that stuff every once in awhile. You can't pay any attention to it." With that, he changed the subject abruptly.

After a time the sobbing stopped.

The following day Terri was off work. Shortly after breakfast, as Ted and Pete walked out into the yard, Gary Bordon came out of the barn leading two saddled horses. Both boys knew immediately what was going to take place. They grinned at each other and winked.

"Is Terri around?" Gary asked, looking at Pete.

"She ought to be out in a few minutes."

Gary grinned. "Wasn't I lucky to have the same day off as she's got? We're going on a picnic up in the hills."

Ted was looking at the bow and the quiver filled

Be Careful, Terri!

with arrows that Terri's friend had slung over his back.

"Just exactly where are you planning to go on that picnic of yours?" Ted asked coldly. "And what are you going to be doing?"

The other boy's grin died. "I wasn't aware of the fact that I had to answer to you when I date Terri. I thought you were her brother, not her dad."

Ted's cheeks colored, but he did not back down. "You don't have to answer to me about Terri. It's up to her whether she wants to go with you or not, but I'm interested in those arrows and the bow you're carrying. Don't you know that the bow-and-arrow season isn't open now?"

Gary laughed, and Ted thought he detected a slight tone of sarcasm in his voice. "You don't think I'd shoot anything out of season, do you?"

"We don't know whether you'd shoot anything out of season or not," Pete broke in quickly, "but we do know what'll happen to you if you get caught doing it."

"I suppose you'd squeal on me."

"You can just bet I would, and so would Pete. We'd have the game warden on you as soon as we could reach a phone. That's a promise."

The color left Gary's cheeks. "Well, you can relax. I just brought the bow along for kicks. I thought maybe we might like to do a little target shooting before we get back."

Ted's eyes narrowed. He didn't know much about archery, and he didn't know the pull of the bow that Gary was carrying; but it looked heavier than the average target bow. And it wasn't anything that Terri could even think of using. He doubted if she could even draw it, let alone hold it steady enough to hit what she was aiming at.

"Let me take a look at one of those arrows, will you?"

Gary pretended that he didn't know the reason for Ted's request. "Sure thing." He reached around behind and pulled one of the arrows out of the quiver. "What do you want to do? Are you going out with us, or are you thinking about taking up archery yourself?"

Ted did not answer him directly. "This *is* a target arrow," he said to no one in particular.

"Sure it is. What did you expect?"

By that time Terri had joined them. "Hi, I didn't expect to see you so soon, Gary."

"I thought we'd better get an early start. We've got quite a ways to ride, you know."

"Oh, I wasn't complaining." Her smile was warm and reassuring.

They rode off together.

Be Careful, Terri!

Ted and Pete watched the two riders go out of the yard and down the long lane.

"What do you make of that guy?" Pete asked, thoughtfully. "Do you think he's the one who lost that broken arrow that we found the other day?"

Ted frowned. "I was just thinking about that. It could be, but we can't forget that he's got target arrows in his quiver. I've got to say that for him."

Pete kicked a small stone with the toe of his boot. "I know, but just the same, I don't trust that guy. You don't suppose Terri would take him up to that old sheepherder's shack, do you?"

"Oh, she wouldn't do that. She wouldn't do anything that would risk Prince Atlas' life," Ted said quickly. "I know her too well for that."

"She might not even think about it this summer —about the importance of not taking anyone up there, I mean. Maybe she doesn't know that Prince is still around the sheepherder's shack."

Ted frowned. That was something he hadn't thought about. After all, Prince Atlas was now over a year old. She would probably think of him as being able to take care of himself. And of course she probably wouldn't think of Gary as being a threat to the young elk. She just might take him up there to show him Prince, if she did know the young elk was hanging around that area.

Ted looked up quickly, as though hoping to see his sister and her boyfriend still in view.

"Do you suppose we ought to ride after them and warn her?"

"We can't do that," Pete said. "We've got a lot of work that has to be done today. Besides, with the head start they've got, we'd have trouble catching them, anyway."

"I suppose you're right." Ted shaded his eyes with his hand. He didn't know why he disliked and distrusted Gary, but he did. And he wished that Terri wasn't dating the guy.

4

A Vicious Companion

Gary and Terri followed the ranch road for almost an hour before angling up the mountain on a narrow, twisting trail. They forded an icy stream, went through a cattle gate, and angled up the steep incline. After several minutes Gary broke the silence.

"What was eating that brother of yours this morning?"

She shook her head. "I didn't notice anything different about him. He seemed to be about as disagreeable as always." She tried to change the subject, but he came back to Ted.

"I don't know what I've done to make him dislike me the way he does, but he sure acts like he doesn't have any use for me."

She did not answer him. She had asked herself several times why Ted disliked the boys she went with. Deep down inside she knew the reason. It was probably because they weren't Christians. But she knew that she could never explain that to a fellow like Gary.

"He put me through a regular inquisition about my having a bow and some arrows along on this picnic. I guess he thinks that I'm a threat to every animal in Colorado."

"That's just Ted." She shrugged defensively. "If you're around him long enough you'll get used to him."

"That's something I'd have to see," Gary replied. "I don't think I could ever get used to *him*. He's a real pain!"

She scowled. It was one thing for her to criticize Ted, but she didn't like hearing anyone else do it.

They negotiated a particularly narrow stretch of trail that skirted a sheer granite wall. Terri gasped when she saw where they would be going.

"Do you think we ought to risk that?" she asked.

He laughed. "Why not? Somebody rides over it every once in a while without falling off."

"That we know of," she added nervously.

"It's not as bad as all that. Come on, Terri. All we've got to do is hang on. Our horses will do the rest." He stared at her. "Afraid?"

"I'd be lying if I said I'm not."

"I'll go first. All you have to do is start your horse behind mine. Then you can close your eyes

A Vicious Companion

and hang onto the saddle horn. You'll be across before you know it. These mountain horses are used to trails like this. They can make it without any sweat."

She said nothing more until they were safely on the other side. Then she sighed her relief, looked back, and shivered. "I'm glad that's over," she murmured aloud.

Gary laughed. "It's over for now, that is."

"For now?" she echoed, eyes widening. "What do you mean by that?"

"Well, we've crossed that cliff once, but when we go back home we're going to have to cross it again. Didn't you think of that?"

"Oh, Gary!"

"But it won't be for quite a while anyway. You can forget it for now."

"I think I'd just as soon go back over it right away and have it over with."

"Don't be silly. It won't be nearly as bad the second time."

When they were once more on the trail, he turned the conversation back to her brother once more. "That brother of yours must be some sort of a nut, the way I get it. I've never known anyone so hard to live with. He acts like he even hates himself."

Terri straightened stiffly. "He's not so bad when you get to know him."

"*If* you can get to know him."

Terri bristled. "Let's not discuss him anymore. OK?"

The hush between them was uncomfortable. Gary saw that he had irritated Terri so he began talking about anything he could think of.

"I'd sure like to get up close to an elk while I'm here this summer," he said.

"I was close to an elk last summer. In fact I had one eating sugar out of my hand."

He didn't believe her. "Sure, in a zoo some place."

"For your information, it wasn't a zoo. In fact, we're not too far from the place right now."

"You're putting me on."

Indignantly she drew herself erect. "If you don't want to believe me, that's your privilege; but I'm telling you the truth. Pete Ellison found this little elk calf. I guess somebody had shot the poor little animal's mother. Pete named him Prince Atlas and took care of the calf himself. By the time Prince was big enough to be on his own, he was tame. We could walk right up to him."

Gary's curiosity glittered in his eyes. "Is that the truth?"

"It certainly is." She went on to tell him how the

elk had gotten wire-cut and almost died, and how Ted had torn down the fence after the elk's leg was well enough so he didn't have to be treated anymore.

"I sure wish I'd known about him last year," Gary said wistfully. "Do you suppose he's still around?"

"That was the first thing Ted asked about when we got back out here this summer. Pete said that he'd seen him several times. I think he must have stayed in the same general area where he had been kept in the fence."

Gary's eyes gleamed. "How far is it over there?"

She didn't like the tone in his voice or the look in his eyes. "It's quite a ways."

"We've got all day," he told her. "We could make it over there easy and still get back long before dark."

She hesitated. She had given her word not to tell anyone about Prince Atlas, or where he was, but that had been the year before. There couldn't be any harm in telling Gary about him now.

"When I got home last year you should have heard the gang razz me because I hadn't seen any wild animals all summer. They told me that I didn't need to come back if I didn't see anything besides rabbits this year." He leaned forward earnestly.

"Won't you take me over there and show him to me, Terri? Please?"

Still she hesitated.

"I won't tell anyone."

"I don't know. I promised that I wouldn't let *anyone* know where Prince is."

"That was a year ago. He may not even be in the area. But it won't hurt to tell *me*. *I* won't let anyone else know about him."

"Why do you want to see him?" she asked.

"Why does anybody want to see anything?" He sounded as though he was getting impatient. "I've never seen a real live elk outside of a zoo or a park, for one thing. And for another, I just happen to like animals and enjoy seeing them in their natural environment. Is that reason enough?"

Her determination to keep the location of the sheepherder's shack a secret began to weaken slightly. "If I do take you over there, will you promise that you won't tell anyone where it is? Not even Sam?"

"You can count on me. I won't tell anybody. As far as I'm concerned, we're just on a little ride in the mountains, and we aren't going any place special. That's all anybody is going to know."

In that moment she decided that it would be all right for her to share the secret with Gary. After all, she had made her promise to Ted a year before, and

Prince Atlas was practically grown now. No harm could come from taking Gary over to the sheepherder's shack in the hope that he would be able to see the young elk.

"You can tell Sam about it after you leave here, if you want to," Terri said, "but I wish you wouldn't say anything to him now."

"It's as good as done. I won't say a word to him or anyone."

Terri wasn't sure whether she remembered the way to the sheepherder's shack. She had only been up there a few times, and they had approached it from a slightly different direction. But she thought she could find it. There weren't too many trails in the area. They turned up the next trail, forded a mountain stream, and headed for the broad expanse of pasture land that the shack was close to.

"I'm counting on the fact that you aren't going to tell anyone else about this."

"How many times do I have to tell you that I'm not going to spill it to anyone?" He acted irritated that she didn't seem to trust him.

It didn't seem to her to take nearly as long for the two of them to get to the sheepherder's place as it had when she rode up there with Ted the summer before. They crossed still another stream and rode up the tortuously steep trail.

"How long ago was it that Pete saw that tame elk of his?" Gary wanted to know.

"I can't answer that for sure. I think he said he had seen him a few days before we got to the ranch this summer. And he and Ted went out to look for him the other day. All they saw were some tracks, though."

"Maybe the elk isn't around anymore," Gary said, disappointedly. "I don't suppose I would ever be lucky enough to see him."

"Who knows? We may be luckier than you think."

Gary's thin body tensed as he leaned forward, peering into the brush on either side of the trail with an intentness that was growing with each passing moment.

"Are we getting close?" he asked in a low, excited voice.

"We're not very far away, as nearly as I can remember it." She paused for a moment. "But I don't know for sure. I was only up here a few times."

"We'd better be quiet," Gary whispered. "We don't want to scare him."

They rode on silently for several minutes. At last they reached the clearing with the ramshackle buildings along the far edge. Terri reined in and dismounted slowly.

A Vicious Companion

"Is this the place we've been looking for?" her companion whispered.

She put a warning finger to her lips.

The two started to walk forward as quietly as possible. A full minute passed, and they saw nothing except a jay chattering raucously to himself.

"I think we might as well go," Gary said, his disappointment keen. "There's no elk around here today."

Then, as though on cue, Prince Atlas stepped into the clearing majestically, his youthful rack held high.

"There he is!" Gary exclaimed in a hoarse whisper. "Just look at him. Isn't he beautiful?"

Terri was staring at the young bull elk so hard that she did not notice what Gary was doing until he stepped forward stealthily.

"Gary!"

"Sh!" He had already notched a hunting arrow and was drawing it back with great deliberation.

"Gary!" This time she almost wailed.

The elk's head jerked quickly in alarm. But it was too late! Gary had already loosed the arrow!

5

A Broken Friendship

As Gary loosed the arrow, Terri screamed, "Run, Prince! *Run! Ru-u-n!*"

The arrow sped straight for the startled young bull; but inches before it reached its target, it nudged a tree branch and ricocheted harmlessly off into the forest. Prince whirled and charged into the brush safely out of sight.

Gary turned on Terri, anger blazing in his eyes. "Now see what you made me do! Why couldn't you have kept your big mouth shut for another half a second? I could have had him! If you'd only kept still, I could have had him!"

"You said you just wanted to take a look at him!" Terri exclaimed. "You said you only wanted to see a wild elk. You didn't say anything at all about wanting to shoot him!" She was even more furious than Gary. "You lied to me!"

His lips parted as though to speak, but he

A Broken Friendship

stopped suddenly. Strangely enough, Prince Atlas had only run a few yards. He turned and came back, bewildered by what had happened. Terri could see him standing near the edge of the clearing, his head held high, his nose testing the wind. He still hadn't learned that men could be dangerous to him.

"Run!" she yelled, waving her arms at him.

Briefly Gary stared at the elk, as confused as Prince Atlas for one tense instant. Then he reached quickly for another hunting arrow. He had to fumble for a moment to find them among the target arrows. The moment he touched the quiver Terri darted forward and snatched the arrows from it. Gary cried out in anger, but he was too late. In one quick movement, she dropped the arrows to the ground and stomped on them, breaking most of them.

"Now look what you've done!" He tried to shove her away.

"Now you aren't going to be able to shoot him!" she shouted triumphantly.

At the first sound of commotion the young elk dashed away.

Gary had tried to push Terri away from the arrows, but he had been too late. She broke all but one of the hunting arrows, and she managed to bend the point on it. He stared at the broken arrows at her feet and then up into her blazing eyes. He was breathing hard and his face was livid with rage.

"And just why did you do that?" he demanded, his voice ominously quiet.

She was so angry she no longer cared what he thought or said. "I told you that I couldn't let you kill Prince. That was the only way I knew how to get you to stop trying."

"I'll show you whether I can shoot him or not!" he exclaimed angrily. "I was just fooling a minute ago, but now I mean business. I'll kill that elk of yours if it's the last thing I ever do."

"But you can't!" she cried, her voice going higher. "It's against the law! Don't you dare try to shoot him again!"

He laughed viciously. "You just watch! You'll find out that you can't stop me."

Terri's concern grew. She had broken the trust Ted placed in her by telling Gary about Prince Atlas. Now Gary claimed that he was going to kill him!

"I don't know what enjoyment you would get out of that. Prince is tame. Shooting him wouldn't be any harder or any more fun than shooting a dog or a cow or a horse. There wouldn't be any sport to it."

"What do you know about it?" He was so angry his face was contorted. "I'd have had him! I'd have

A Broken Friendship

had him easy with that first arrow if you hadn't yelled so loud you spoiled my aim. I've made a lot of shots that were longer and harder than that one. It was your fault that I didn't get that elk!"

"I'm *glad* I made you miss him," she retorted defiantly. "I'm *real* glad I made you miss him. I'd do it again if I got the chance."

"You're not going to get another chance. Now, what do you think of that?" He pulled in a deep breath and expelled it with a rush. "I'm going to make you a promise, Terri Walker, and I want you to remember it good. I'm going to kill that elk of yours before I go back home."

She stared at him as though someone had ripped away the blindfold from her eyes, and for the first time she was seeing what he was actually like.

"If you do, I'll see that you're arrested and punished for it. There are laws against hunting out of season, you know."

"You'll have to prove it first. You'll know that I killed that precious Prince Atlas of yours, but you won't be able to prove it."

Suddenly she felt that she couldn't stand to be with him for another minute. "I think you'd better take me home, Gary," she told him coldly.

He glared at her. "That's the best thing you've said today!"

They mounted their horses and rode back toward

the ranch. For some time they rode in silence, each lost in his own thoughts.

"I suppose this puts an end to your going to the Eagle's Nest with me," Gary said. Strangely enough, his voice softened slightly, and Terry thought he sounded disappointed.

"It certainly does," she retorted. "I wouldn't go anywhere with you again. I don't care how badly I might want to go where you'd take me."

Now she didn't have to worry about going to the Eagle's Nest with him. That matter was all taken care of. She meant it when she said that she wasn't going any place with Gary anymore! For once Ted was right about one of the fellows she had been going with.

"I don't know what was the matter with me," he told her, fumbling for words. "I shouldn't have done that. I just got carried away. I've shot a lot of rabbits with my bow, but I've never had a chance to shoot a big animal before. I shouldn't have tried a stupid trick like that."

"You're a little late to be coming to that conclusion, aren't you?" she asked. "You not only shot at him, you got mad because I interfered."

Gary began to realize the situation he had placed himself in with Terri. "I don't really think I could have shot Prince Atlas," he continued. "Now that I think of it, I know I couldn't. He meant so much to

A Broken Friendship

you that I couldn't have killed him, no matter how badly I may have wanted to."

She was so angry that her very being trembled. "You'll never make me buy that, Gary, so just save your breath. You lied to me about why you wanted to come over here in the first place. Then when you saw Prince you did everything you could do to kill him and were furious at me when I stopped you by breaking your arrows!"

He looked at her sheepishly. "What can I do to make you see how sorry I am?"

"Nothing!" Her voice was like ice. "There's absolutely nothing you can do."

6

A New Plan of Action

Terri rode in silence, ignoring her companion as much as possible. He tried to apologize to her for what he had done, but she was still so angry she refused to accept it.

"I know you must think I'm an awful heel," he began, "but you wouldn't, if you would just let me explain. It isn't nearly as bad as it seems to be, and that's the truth."

"As far as I'm concerned," she retorted haughtily, "the conversation is over. There's nothing more for you to explain. Let's just forget it. OK?"

When he saw that it was useless trying to talk with her, his anger surged back. "All right! If that's the way you feel about it, we'll forget the whole thing. I've tried to explain to you, but you won't listen. So go ahead and be mad at me. I can get along without you."

A New Plan of Action 49

"I'm relieved to know that."

He shook his head. "I never saw anyone so disagreeable."

As for Terri, all that concerned her was to get far from Gary as quickly as possible. He wasn't to be trusted, she had learned. And, as far as she was concerned, she wasn't going to give him another opportunity to prove himself. He had already shown her his true colors. She was extremely glad that Prince was still alive. If Gary had had his way, he wouldn't be.

Ted was working near the barn when Terri and her companion came riding in. He read the anger in his twin sister's eyes and went quickly out to meet her.

"What's the matter, Terri?" he demanded. "Is there anything wrong?"

"Of course not," Gary snapped. "There's nothing wrong!"

"I wasn't talking to you."

Gary dismounted and led his horse into the barn, not even waiting for Terri.

"What is the trouble, Terri?" Ted asked. "That character didn't give you a hard time, did he?"

"There isn't anything wrong," she repeated nervously. "At least not the way you think. But he burns me up!"

Ted shook his head in bewilderment. He ought to

quit trying to understand that sister of his. He never could figure her out. He was still staring after her when Pete came up to him.

"What's the deal? Terri looks like a storm about to happen."

"Search me. She claims there's nothing wrong, but I know that look in her eyes. She's awful mad!"

A few moments later Terri came out of the barn, walked past them angrily and stormed up to the house.

Both boys watched until the screen door slammed behind her.

"I ought to go up and talk to her," Ted murmured, "but the mood she's in, she probably wouldn't tell me anything anyway."

Terri was glad that Mrs. Ellison was not in the house when she went in. She did not want to talk to anyone right then. All she wanted was to be alone. She hurried up to her room and closed the door behind her.

For several minutes Terri stood before the bedroom window, looking out at Bald Mountain where the young elk was living unsuspectingly. Tears of anger trickled down her cheeks, but she made no sound. She stood motionless, her breath coming in thin, shallow drafts, her eyes dull and expressionless.

A New Plan of Action

She had ruined everything by breaking Ted's confidence and telling Gary about Prince Atlas and where he could be found. He tried to make her believe that he hadn't intended to kill the young elk, but she knew better. Now that he knew where Prince was, he would go back and try again. She was sure of that. If for no other reason, he'd do it just to show her that he could. And when that happened, it would be her fault.

Standing at the window she began to pray a desperate, silent prayer for help.

Dear God, I've messed things up again, she prayed silently. *I told Gary about Pete's elk pet, and now I know that he's going to go back and— and shoot him. And he's so tame it will be easy to get close enough to kill him with an arrow. Dear God, please chase the elk away and make him afraid of people so he won't come out as boldly as he does.*

She was still praying when there was a light knock on her door.

"Terri, can I come in?" Ted asked softly.

She opened the door. "What do you want?" There was an edge to her voice.

"Are you all right?"

She closed the door to keep their voices from the other part of the house. "Of course I'm all right. Why wouldn't I be?"

"You were sure mad when you came back. I thought maybe you and Gary had a big argument."

She wasn't angry at her brother, but she bristled at what she considered his prying. "And what if we did? Is that any business of yours?"

"Don't be like that. I just want to help, if I can."

Her eyes softened. "I'm sorry, Ted, but I'm so upset right now I don't know what I'm saying."

Sitting down at her desk, she told him what had taken place on the ride.

"And—I just know that he's not going to give up until he's had another try at killing Prince." She breathed deeply. "But there's nothing I can do about it. That's the worst part."

Ted masked his own concern. "He probably wouldn't be able to hit Prince if he could find him again and get close enough to take a shot. Most bow-and-arrow hunters come back empty-handed."

"You don't know how good he is with that bow," Terri continued. "I think he would have killed Prince with the first shot if I hadn't yelled and spoiled his aim."

Ted frowned thoughtfully. "I didn't even think he had any hunting arrows. The one I looked at had a target point. He must have had them mixed in his quiver."

"He sure had them when he wanted them. I can tell you that much."

A New Plan of Action

"What do you want me to do?"

She shook her head. "I don't know whether there's anything anybody can do." She got up nervously and paced to the window and back. "It won't do any good to try to talk with him. He won't listen to anybody. I've never talked with anyone who's got such a thing about killing something with a bow and arrow. He acted like he's blown his mind."

Ted stood still and silent. He didn't know for sure what could be done about Gary. It wouldn't do any good to try to talk with him about it; he wouldn't listen to anybody. And if he did agree to leave Prince alone, it wouldn't mean anything. He'd only lie about it, if he thought it would suit his purpose. No, they had to come up with something else.

He studied his sister's somber face. He couldn't let Terri worry about Prince Atlas, even if it was her fault that his life was in danger. "Don't worry about it," he said. "I'll talk it over with Pete. We'll come up with something."

She smiled, wiping her tears. "You're the best brother a girl ever had."

He grinned. "You're just saying that because you know it's true."

Pete was more disturbed than either Ted or Terri when he learned what had taken place.

"I don't trust that guy. I don't trust him at all."

"Neither do I. That's why I thought I ought to talk with you about it and see what we can work out. I don't think there's any doubt that he's going to be out there every chance he gets, trying to get a shot at Prince."

Pete sighed deeply and stared wistfully up at the mountain. "There's got to be something we can do, but what? That's the thing that's got me puzzled."

They talked for an hour, trying to decide what to do about it.

"Maybe we ought to try talking," Pete said. "That's all I can think of that would have any chance of working."

"He'll only laugh at us. And even if he doesn't, we can't know whether he means what he says or if he's lying to us."

Pete thought about that. What Ted said was true. You couldn't depend on anything Gary said.

"But we might be able to scare him good. We can let him know that we're keeping a close tab on Prince; and if he's hurt in any way, we're going to get the game warden on him."

"It may work," Ted replied doubtfully.

"It's *got* to work." His mouth tightened firmly. "We'll start out by letting him know that we're telling the truth when we say that."

"What do you mean?"

"I'll talk to Dad and make arrangements for you

A New Plan of Action

and me to get off tomorrow afternoon to ride up to the old sheepherder's place and make up the time later. We'll let Gary know where we're going and why. That'll be a good start."

Ted nodded. "He hasn't had a chance to get up there again since he and Terri went up there on their picnic."

That night before going to bed Ted and Pete prayed together briefly, asking God to help Prince to avoid Gary Bordon's arrows.

"And, Lord, help Prince to get so afraid of people that he won't let anyone get close enough to shoot him." Pete said.

When they finished praying, they both felt a bit better than they had before.

"Ted, I'm just beginning to realize how wrong I was in taming that little elk," Pete said. "Terri feels awful about Gary finding out where Prince is; and if anything happens to him, she'd blame herself for it. But, you know, I'm the one who's really to blame." He drew in a long breath and expelled the air slowly. "If it hadn't been for me, Prince would have grown up as wild and as shy as any of the other elk in the area. He wouldn't be so tame that anybody with a bow and arrow could get close enough to shoot him."

Ted ran his hand across his face in a nervous gesture. What Pete said was true, only he had never thought of it in quite that way. But there was something else that was true as well. In his particular case, at least. Pete alone was not responsible, nor Terri either. He got to his feet uneasily.

"When it comes to taking the blame, I've got to share it, too."

"You?" Pete looked up. "What could you have possibly done to have been responsible for this situation?"

Ted went to the window and looked out at the starry sky. "I met Gary and Sam last summer and I saw plenty of them. They both spent a lot of time over at your place calling on Terri. But I never once talked with either one of them about their need of the Lord Jesus Christ. If I had witnessed to them the way I should have, they might be followers of Christ now. And if they were, we wouldn't have to worry about Gary shooting Prince Atlas out of season."

Pete thought about that. He had only been a believer about a year so he didn't know for sure whether Ted was being unnecessarily hard on himself or not. But what Ted had said just now made sense. He knew his own attitude had changed a lot about things in general after he decided to follow the Lord.

"Maybe we're planning to talk with Gary about the wrong things," he said.

A New Plan of Action

Ted stared at him. "What do you mean?"

"Maybe we ought to be talking with him about his need for taking the Lord Jesus Christ into his life."

Ted pulled in a deep breath. He didn't know what had been the matter with him. He had just realized the mistake he had made in not witnessing to Gary. Now he was making the same mistake. It wouldn't be easy to talk with Gary about his need for Christ. It never was easy to talk with a guy like him who thought he knew it all. But it was something he had to do. There was no other choice.

"You're right about that, Pete. I'll talk to him. But we'll have to do a lot of praying first."

Lying in bed that night, Ted had great difficulty in getting to sleep. He kept going over and over in his mind what he would say to Gary Bordon.

7

New Problems

Terri usually lingered in the dining hall for a few minutes after getting off work in the evening. She did it hopefully, expecting Gary or Sam to come over to talk for a while or to have a coke with her. And if neither of them showed, she could usually count on one of the guys who came to the ranch as a guest to want to visit with her.

On most nights she looked forward to that hour or so after the day's work was done. On this particular occasion, however, she went back to the Ellison home as soon as she finished work. She was anxious to avoid everyone. She didn't think that she could stand listening to their small talk.

She went directly to her room and closed the door, not even wanting to talk to Ted or Pete.

Shortly before ten o'clock, however, Sam came to see her. She came down from her room at Mrs. Ellison's call, frowning her displeasure.

New Problems

"Hi, I'll bet you didn't expect to see me again this evening." His grin was broad.

"As a matter of fact I didn't."

"Well, you can relax. I'm here."

"It's much too late to go anywhere tonight," she informed him.

"I know that." He moistened his lips nervously. "I just stopped by to talk with you for a minute or two."

"All right, but please hurry. I want to get to bed."

He cleared his throat. "I was just talking to Gary. You might not know it, but he's awful mad at you. I've never seen him so mad at anyone in my whole life."

She didn't show any reaction. "You surely didn't come all the way up here to tell me that, did you? That doesn't disturb me in the least."

"Then you will go with me to the Eagle's Nest to hear Harry's Apes Thursday night?" he asked hopefully.

She stared at him. When she and Gary had fought over the little elk and she refused to go to the nightclub with him, she thought the problem was over and done with. She hadn't expected Sam to come and ask to take her to the same place.

"You can't get reservations," she informed him.

"I've already got them." His eyes sparkled. "It

wasn't easy, but I turned on the old charm and managed to get a couple. How about it? You'll go with me, won't you?"

She hesitated, staring numbly at him. Now she was faced with the same problem as before.

"I—I don't know."

"You always said that I rated as well with you as Gary did," he reminded her. "You said that you couldn't choose between us."

"I know."

"Was it true, or wasn't it?"

"Of course it was true. I enjoy going with both of you."

"Then how about it? Will you go with me to the Eagle's Nest?"

She swallowed hard. "I don't think I can do that, Sam. I'm sorry."

His face clouded. "And why not? Answer me that."

She had to have some reason for not going with him, some reason other than because she didn't care to go with him. He would be more angry at her than Gary was now if she flatly refused to date him.

"What's your reason, Terri?"

"I—I don't feel well at all." The words just slipped out. She had done it again! She had lied!

Sam stared suspiciously at her. "I don't know whether to buy that or not."

New Problems

"Maybe you don't, but it so happens that I'm telling you the truth."

"You were going with Gary until you two had a fight about that elk. Explain that to me, if you can."

She drew herself erect, haughtily. "I don't have to explain anything to you. I hope you realize that." She took half a step backward. "Now, if you'll excuse me, I really have to get to bed." She marched up the stairs to her room and closed the door decisively behind her.

She didn't know what was the matter with her. She hadn't wanted to lie to Sam. She hadn't intended to. It just popped out.

That night she lay restlessly on her bed, turning and twisting as though sleep would never come. Now she had lost both Gary and Sam, and she hadn't been completely honest with either of them. She closed her eyes tightly and prayed for forgiveness, but it didn't seem as though God had heard her prayers.

* * *

The following morning as soon as breakfast was over, Ted and Pete set to work eagerly, determined to get as much done as possible before they took off for the afternoon.

"How are you going to go about talking to Gary?" Pete asked, curiously. He knew how Ted had approached him, but that was all he did know. He had never tried to talk with anyone about his need of the Lord Jesus Christ, and he wasn't at all sure how to go about it.

Ted looked up slowly, concern expressed on his face. "I haven't figured that out yet," he murmured. "I was awake half of last night trying to figure that out; but I still don't have the slightest clue as to how to begin, or what to say after I do start talking to him." He glanced at his watch without any particular reason. "I suppose the first thing I'll have to do is to get him off by himself."

Pete grinned. "That part isn't going to be so tough. Here he comes now. I'll split so you two can be alone."

Ted's tongue thickened and his mouth was dry. He had been about to ask him to stay; but before he was able to, Pete had gone, leaving him to face Gary alone.

"Hi."

The other boy did not acknowledge his greeting. "Where's Terri? I haven't been able to find her anywhere."

"She's working, I suppose. At least that's where she was when I saw her last."

Gary's eyes narrowed as though he half suspected that Ted was telling him something that wasn't true.

New Problems

"I was over at the dining hall just now, but I didn't see her there."

Ted was about to suggest that perhaps Terri saw Gary first, but he didn't. There was no use in antagonizing him. "She ought to be off work in a little while," he said.

Gary turned and started away, but Ted called to him.

"I'd like to talk to you for a minute, if you've got time."

Gary came back reluctantly. "I suppose it's about what happened yesterday," he answered with belligerence.

"Not exactly. I wanted to talk to you about yourself." He was fumbling for words frantically, trying to get hold of an approach that would catch Gary's interest.

"And just exactly what's wrong with me?" the other boy demanded. "What have I done now that makes me such an outlaw?"

"It isn't that," Ted said. He didn't know why, but he always felt at a disadvantage when he tried to talk with someone about his soul. "It's just that I've been doing a lot of thinking about you lately." He took a deep breath. "Have you ever considered the claim the Lord Jesus Christ has on your life?"

Gary stared at him as though he had never heard

anything quite like that before and he wasn't sure he heard Ted correctly. "What did you say?"

"I've been wondering if anyone has ever talked with you about the Lord Jesus Christ." Ted went on, sweat standing out on his forehead. "Did you know that He loves you so much that He died on the cross to save you?"

"I don't go much for that kind of talk. To tell you the truth, I've never had much use for religion."

"To tell you the truth I've never cared much for religion either," Ted replied. "But I'm not talking about religion; I'm talking about a Person, Someone who can forgive your sin and give you a completely new life."

Gary remained motionless, staring incredulously at him. "I—I—" he stammered frantically. "I've got to be going. Mr. Ellison will skin me alive if I don't get my work done today."

"I'd like to finish talking with you," Ted told him. "Could I see you tonight after dinner?"

Gary was edging for the door. "I don't know. I mean, I don't think so. I've got a lot of things to do tonight. I don't think I could make it." With that, he backed away and was gone, hurrying in the direction of the house.

Ted stared after him, the numbness still holding him in its grip. He still had not moved when Pete came up beside him.

New Problems

"That didn't take very long."

"It certainly didn't." There was a faraway tone in his voice.

"Did you get a chance to talk to him?"

"I got a chance to start talking to him," Ted answered. "But as soon as he realized that I wanted to tell him about Jesus Christ, he went scooting out of here like a scared rabbit."

Pete had been hopeful that Ted would be able to lead Gary to Christ and solve the problem of Prince Atlas in that way. Now he realized that they were going to have to do something else.

"Did you let him know where we're going this afternoon?"

Ted shook his head. "No, but I will. You can be sure of that."

That afternoon Ted and Pete saddled their horses and rode hurriedly over to the sheepherder's shack on Bald Mountain. The nearer they got to the place where Prince Atlas had been seen last, the more tense they became.

"I'm sure Gary hasn't had a chance to get back up here again."

"So am I."

"Just the same, I'll feel a lot better when we see Prince and find out that he's all right."

Ted nodded. He agreed with Pete about Gary.

He didn't see how he could possibly have gotten back to the old shack.

They rode on for several minutes.

"I sure don't know what fun that character would get out of shooting a tame elk with a bow. I haven't started hunting yet," Ted went on, "but I'll bet that when I do, I won't get excited about killing a tame animal. What sort of an accomplishment would that be, anyway? Answer me that."

His companion shrugged. What kind of a person could enjoy killing an animal so tame that he wouldn't protect himself?

8

A New Threat

They rode on up the steep trail to the clearing where the old sheepherder had built his shack years before. For a minute or so they sat motionless on their ponies, looking about for some sign of Prince. But he was nowhere around.

"I don't see him," Ted said, trying to sound casual. "Do you?"

Pete shook his head. "Maybe he's roamed away for a few days. He does that every once in a while, you know."

"I was thinking about that myself."

Pete dismounted and dropped the reins so his well-trained saddle horse would stand still. "Gary could have gotten back here, after all. I'll never forgive myself if he did get to Prince."

"I don't think we should worry too much about it yet," Ted went on. "The fact that we don't see him right now doesn't mean that he's been killed. You remember how it was the last time we were up here. We didn't see him then either, but Terri and Gary did when they came. So, this doesn't mean anything."

"Maybe not." But the sound of his voice revealed that he thought it did mean a great deal.

Pete found the arrows that Terri had broken. Four of them were target arrows and the rest were broadhead hunting arrows. In spite of the seriousness of the situation, he grinned.

"Terri sure fixed Bordon, didn't she? She must have broken every arrow he had."

Ted took one of the broken arrows from his friend's hand and began to examine it thoughtfully. "What did you do with that other hunting arrow?" he asked. "The broken one that you and I found up here?"

Pete shrugged. "I don't remember. I guess I just threw it down when we finished looking at it. Why?"

"I'd just like to find it and look at it again, that's all."

"What for?"

"Come on and help me find it." Ted moved in the direction of the area where he had found the broken hunting arrow on their last trip.

"What do you hope to prove with it?"

"Maybe nothing. But it seems to me that the

A New Threat

arrows Terri broke are quite different from the one we found here the other day. I thought I'd like to take a squint at it and see if I'm right."

Pete couldn't understand the purpose for the search. "I still don't get it."

Ted straightened. "I've always understood that most archers find the brand of arrows they like and stay with them."

Pete's eyes widened. "That's right! I don't know why I didn't think of it before." He straightened slowly and stared beyond his companion at the distant hills. "If the arrows are different, that would prove that Gary wasn't up here the other time after all."

"That's right. And the way I see it, it would mean there's someone *else* who's trying to kill Prince with a bow, too."

Pete bit his lower lip nervously. "Then we've got *two* guys to worry about instead of one."

"I hadn't thought of it that way."

A few moments later Ted found the other arrow. It was entirely different than the arrows Terri had broken for Gary.

"They aren't the same, are they?" Pete asked.

Ted shook his head. "Nope. And as far as I'm concerned, there's no doubt about it. There is somebody else besides Borden who's after Prince!"

"We get back to that same old question. What are we going to do about it?"

That was what had been bothering Ted. They would have a difficult time keeping track of Gary and trying to see that he didn't get up to the sheepherder's and put an arrow in Prince. Now they had another fellow to be concerned about. And they didn't know who he was or where he came from or whether he would come back. They didn't have a chance of trying to stop him.

Ted started to throw the broken arrow away, but changed his mind and put it in his saddlebag. "You know, Pete, I just thought of something. There's nothing we can do about stopping any hunters who might want to get off a shot at Prince, but maybe there's something we can do about *him*."

"I don't follow you."

"Maybe we can make him so afraid of people that he won't come near anyone."

Pete paused, the corners of his mouth tightening. "You might have a point at that."

"There ought to be something we could do."

Pete's eyes brightened. "Why don't we bring a rifle up here and shoot at him a few times?"

Ted gasped. "*Shoot* at him? Are you out of your mind?"

"I don't mean that we ought to shoot him—or even aim at him. I just thought the sound of the gun

A New Threat

might be enough to scare him back into the woods and make him afraid of people. It looks as though he's been shot at a couple of times with arrows, but they don't make any noise. He wouldn't know that he's being shot at."

Ted kicked a small rock with the toe of his boot. There had to be an answer to their problem—a better answer than a high-powered rifle. Besides, the rifle could get them into trouble if someone caught them shooting it. They'd never be able to convince the authorities that they were just shooting to scare Prince.

Then it came to him. "You know," he began thoughtfully, "I think I'm getting an idea. If only there was some way we could get a hold of some firecrackers."

"My dad gets a good supply of fireworks every year and invites all the neighbors in for a barbecue on the Fourth of July. The fireworks are the entertainment for the evening."

"Have the fireworks come yet?"

"I think so. He probably brought them from Denver the last time he went in." Pete's eyes brightened with excitement.

"If we can talk your dad out of a dozen big firecrackers—some real blockbusters—we'll be able to scare Prince so bad he'll *never* want to be around humans again."

A wide grin was spreading across Pete's tanned face. "That'll sure do the trick! Let's get a move on so we can get back home and get out here again before dark."

"Think we can make it?" Ted asked. "That's quite a long ride."

"Maybe we can't, but we can get some of our work out of the way so we can be sure and get back up here tomorrow or the next day."

* * *

Terri didn't see Gary all that day. Actually, she didn't care to see him at all; and if she had known he would have been waiting for her just outside the kitchen door when she got off work in the evening, she would have gone out another way. But there he was. She had to talk with him.

"Hello, Terri." His voice was warm and conciliatory. "I'm glad I got to see you tonight."

"There's no point in our seeing each other." Her gaze met his. "We have nothing whatever to discuss."

"Don't be like that. I've just got to talk with you." He sounded genuine, as though he was telling her the truth. "I feel terrible about what happened yesterday, so I came over to apologize. I'm terribly sorry about what I did. I don't want to keep on fighting with you."

"You should have thought of that yesterday."

A New Threat

He ignored the harshness in her voice. "I thought I'd come over and talk with you about our date for Thursday night."

She drew herself erect. "Date?" she echoed. "There must be some mistake. I wasn't aware of the fact that we still have a date for Thursday night."

He groaned aloud. "Aw, Terri, don't be so uptight about yesterday. We've had so much fun together this summer! We can't quit being friends over somebody's stupid pet elk."

"Perhaps not. Apparently our friendship—I mean, *my* friendship—doesn't mean anything to you. So, I really have nothing more to say."

"Don't be that way!"

"If you've finished," she retorted, "we can conclude this conversation."

Gary shifted uneasily from one foot to the other. "I didn't come here because I want to fight with you," he said. "Believe me."

"Then why did you come?"

"I thought maybe we could make a bargain."

She had been close to pushing past him and hurrying up to the house, but she paused, squinting narrowly into his face. "What kind of a bargain are you talking about?"

"If you'll be friends with me again and go with me to the Eagle's Nest Thursday night to hear Harry's Apes, I'll give you my word that I'll never go back and try to shoot that little elk you're so worried about. I won't even go back to take a look at him."

She brushed a strand of hair away from her eyes. She had expected nothing like this from him. She thought he was going to plead with her to go to the nightclub with him or try to persuade her that she would have so much fun that she wouldn't want to miss it.

Instead, he said he was sorry and offered to make a deal not to try to shoot Prince again. It would be wonderful if she could make an arrangement like that with him. Then she wouldn't have to worry about Prince Atlas, or the fact that she had violated the trust Ted placed in her in telling her about the young elk and asking her to keep it a secret.

But what about Sam? She had told him that she couldn't go with him because she didn't feel well. If she changed her mind now and went with Gary, Sam would be mad at her. So, she'd lose out, no matter what she did.

And too, there was her own conviction against going to a place like that. She tried to make herself believe that it would be all right, but she was only kidding herself, she knew now. She still felt as though it would be wrong for her to go, even to hear the rock group sing.

"I'm sorry, Gary," she said. "I would like to go with you, but I just can't."

A New Threat

He stiffened slightly. "You *can't*? And why not? What sort of an excuse do you have for not going with me this time?"

"It isn't an excuse." Her face was crimson. "It's the truth." The words stabbed into her very being. She had lied again!

Gary's eyes flashed. "You're putting me on!" he blurted belligerently. "Well, you can forget it! And you can forget what I told you about promising not to kill that precious elk of yours, too! I offered you a deal, but you refused, so now you'll have to suffer the consequences!"

With that he whirled and stomped away.

9

New Arrivals

Terri stared after Gary, rapidly becoming more upset.

Why couldn't she have told him the truth? Why couldn't she have told both boys the truth right from the first? She could have explained that she was a Christian and had convictions against doing certain things and going certain places. If she had done that, she would have had no difficulty in letting them know why she didn't feel that she could go to a place like the Eagle's Nest, not even to sit and listen to the music.

But there was something about letting people like Gary and Sam know that she was a believer in the Lord Jesus Christ that was almost impossible for her to do. She couldn't have them thinking that she was a religious fanatic. They already had that idea about Ted. She had heard them laugh at him and ridicule him behind his back. She couldn't have

New Arrivals

them thinking the same thing about her and laughing about her afterward. No good could come of that.

No good could come of her lying either, or of her pretending to be something that she wasn't. The icy lump in her stomach seemed to grow as she closed the door and hurried up to her room.

She really hadn't been sick when she talked to Sam, she had to admit. It had been a lie to get her out of the dilemma she found herself in. But now, as she thought about the lies she had told Sam and Gary in order to keep them from knowing that it was her Christian convictions that were keeping her from going to the Eagle's Nest, her head ached and a great weariness engulfed her. By the time she was ready for bed, nausea gripped her stomach and her head throbbed.

If there had been anyone to take her place at the M-Bar-H the following day, she would have decided right then that she was too ill to go to work and would have stayed in bed. However, Mrs. Ellison had told her that there were several new guests coming the next afternoon; and the dude ranch was already short-handed. If she decided against working she didn't know what the ranch owner's wife would do. So, even though she felt miserable and was sure she would be even worse by morning, she planned to go to work.

The next day she got up when her alarm went off and carried out her duties mechanically, a fixed smile masking the sickness that she felt inside. No matter how hard she tried, nothing seemed to come out right. She wanted to live for the Lord and she wanted to keep the friendship of both Gary and Sam. Now she was losing out all the way around and there didn't seem to be anything she could do about it.

* * *

Pete and Ted wanted to talk with Mr. Ellison about getting some of his bigger firecrackers from him that evening when they got home; but the ranch owner was in town when they returned, and he didn't get back until after they had gone to bed. It was the following morning after breakfast before they got an opportunity to talk to him. Even then they had to follow him out to the yard to get him away from the others.

Mr. Ellison was surprised at their request for firecrackers. He frowned thoughtfully, pushing his hat back on his head with a calloused forefinger.

"There were plenty of big firecrackers on my order this year," he said, "and you can have a few if you want them. But what's this all about? What are you going to do with firecrackers, anyway?"

"We've got a good reason for wanting them."

New Arrivals

Pete had never told his folks about Prince Atlas until that moment. He started at the beginning and told his dad all that had taken place. He told him how he found Prince as a newborn calf the year before and took care of him and tamed him until late summer, when Ted finally was able to convince him that he ought to tear down the fence and let the elk calf go. "But the trouble is, he's too tame for his own good."

"That often happens. It's one of the big reasons it's not wise to tame wild animals. All too often they aren't suited for living out of captivity. Or if they are, they've lost their fear of humans, which can make them a nuisance or a distinct menace to themselves."

"That's what happened with Prince. And two days ago Gary tried to shoot him with a bow and arrow."

An angry frown appeared on Mr. Ellison's face. "The season isn't open for several months. I can keep Gary away from your pet elk. I'll call him in and tell him that I must have a promise from him that he'll leave the young elk alone. If he won't do it, I'll send him home."

"You can't depend on him, Dad. His word doesn't mean a thing."

"He's not going to want to tangle with the game warden. I can assure you of that."

There was a short silence.

"Gary's only part of the trouble," Ted said quietly. "We figured that if he could get close enough to try to shoot Prince with an arrow, some other hunter could do the same. And maybe the next guy will have a gun instead of an arrow."

"That's probably true," Mr. Ellison said, scratching the back of his head.

"So, Dad," Pete continued, "we figure that we've got to do something to make Prince so scared of people that he'll take off when somebody comes his way instead of waiting around to see if he's going to be offered some sugar."

His dad nodded. "I think you've got a point there. So is that why you asked me for firecrackers?"

Ted nodded. "We figure a few well-thrown firecrackers ought to scare Prince Atlas so bad he'll run to the other side of the mountain and won't come back for a week."

"I think you're right. An elk is a smart animal. A few firecrackers will probably give him a very healthy respect for man."

The boys glanced at each other quickly, feeling very relieved.

"Now, if you could get the firecrackers for us and just let us off for a few more hours, we'll give Prince Atlas the scare of his young life."

New Arrivals

"I'd like to let you have the firecrackers now. I know you're anxious to get back up to the sheepherder's cabin and use them. But the truth is that my fireworks haven't come yet."

Pete could scarcely believe him. "But I thought you went in town last night and picked them up!"

"I ordered them and they should have been here a week ago, but they're not. I'm beginning to wonder what happened to them."

Pete groaned. He thought they had solved their problem. Now, however, he realized that Prince Atlas might still be in grave danger. "When do you think they'll come?"

"I don't know. They might be here tomorrow or they might not come for another week."

"A lot of things can happen in a week."

His dad straightened. "I know that, Pete. You should have thought about that before you tamed that elk. There's where the real trouble is."

Dejectedly the boys went out to the barn and set to work, trying to keep from thinking about Prince and the danger he might be in.

"I wish we could ride up there this afternoon and make sure he's all right," Ted told his companion.

"So do I, but we don't have a chance of getting off until those fireworks arrive. I think Dad figures there's nothing we can do until we get those firecrackers."

They had worked an hour or more when a new, dusty station wagon piled high with gear pulled into the ranch yard and stopped. The boys both stared at it.

"Wow!" Ted exclaimed under his breath. "Did you ever see a rig like that?"

"It looks like those new guests Mom and Dad were talking about got here a little early."

The station wagon pulled up to the lodge and stopped. The driver's door opened and a thin, long-haired individual got out and swaggered in the direction of the office. The station wagon looked as though it was crowded with long hair and beards. Rock music blared from the car radio.

Both Ted and Pete watched curiously until the newcomer disappeared from view. "Are you thinking what I'm thinking?" Ted asked softly.

"If you're thinking about the rock group that's singing at the Eagle's Nest this week, and are wondering if we're looking at them, I'd say you're right. I've got a hunch that Harry of Harry's Apes just went into the office to register."

Ted grinned. "Do you think we've *really* and *truly* seen him?" He mimicked his sister.

"In the flesh," Pete said, laughing. With that he picked up a stone and tossed it aside.

"The only thing I can't figure out is why they would come way out here to stay when it would be

New Arrivals

closer for them to go to a motel in town. And it would be a lot handier for them."

Pete shrugged. "We're only twelve miles from the nightclub, for one thing. And for another, they probably want to get a couple of days' rest before they start to work."

Ted wiped his sweating forehead with the back of his hand. "I just thought of something. Those guys furnish Terri with her favorite music. She's *really* going to flip if they really are the Apes."

"Now you've got me curious about them." He lowered his voice to a whisper. "You stay here, Ted. I'm going up and see if they're who we think they are."

Ted turned back to work. He didn't really mind the music of Harry's Apes. They were as good as most singing groups and better than a lot of them. Their music wasn't acid rock like some of the combos and you could understand most of their lyrics. Still he could take them or leave them.

With Terri it was another story. She went silly over their music and would have bought every record they ever made, if she had the money. Ted had been half afraid, when he first saw the ads publicizing the group's appearance at the Eagle's Nest, that Terri would want to go to the nightclub to hear them, but she had said nothing to him about it. Finally he decided that he was underestimating her concern for her Christian testimony.

Ted had just gone back to work when Pete came running back to join him.

"Well, what did you find out?" Ted asked.

"It's them, all right."

"Are they going to be staying here?"

"I guess so. Dad was talking to the guy when I went in. They were the ones who had sent in their reservations."

Ted grinned. "I can hardly wait to see the look on Terri's face when she finds out who they are."

10

The Obnoxious Apes

Ted started to go back to work, but Pete stopped him. "Come on, we've got a job to do."

"Like what?"

"Like carrying about twenty tons of luggage, man. And the sooner we get with it, the sooner the Apes are going to come down out of their trees and relax."

"Maybe I'll get to see them and ask for their autographs."

"*You* after autographs? You wouldn't kid me, would you?" The wide grin on Ted's face answered Pete's questions.

It seemed to Ted that the singers were carrying at least three times the luggage of other people. They made repeated trips from the station wagon to the rooms that had been reserved. There were cameras and fishing rods and golf clubs, and two of the men had expensive laminated bows and two boxes of arrows.

"We're sure having a run on archers this summer," Pete murmured as he pulled the bows from the luggage rack. "I don't know what's going on, but the bow-and-arrow people are getting awfully popular all of a sudden."

Ted looked up, his face darkening. "I can tell you one thing. I'd sure like to tromp on that box of arrows the way Terri did."

Pete's frown deepened. "I know exactly how you feel, but I don't think we would make the M-Bar-H very popular with those guys if we broke their arrows."

"I can dream, can't I?"

"Maybe they're only interested in target shooting. From what I understand most archers don't even consider going into hunting."

Ted scanned the bow he was carrying. Even though he wasn't an expert, he knew that he had a hunting bow in his hands. It was shorter and heavier than the average.

"This isn't target equipment, Pete," he whispered softly. "I can tell you that right now. This bow's got a fifty-pound pull. I'd give a lot to look into this box of arrows and see what kind they are."

"So would I. But we can't do that. They don't belong to us."

The Obnoxious Apes

At that moment one of the bearded, long-haired strangers came bustling up to them. "Hey, you guys! Get with it! We haven't got all day to wait on you!"

"We'll be right with you," Pete said.

The boys picked up a load of gear and started for the lodge where the six entertainers were staying. Unloading everything was the work of ten or fifteen minutes. They still had not finished when the spokesman of the group approached. He came strutting up to them with a smirk that was infuriating.

"I suppose you know who we are."

Ted nodded. "We sort of figured that you're the group that's appearing at the Eagle's Nest the last of this week and the first of next."

"That's right. We've given them a week. A whole *week*. Don't usually stay in one place that long. We've got our public to think of. They keep demanding our appearance all over the country."

Ted and Pete were trying to think of something to say to him when he continued.

"That's right. We're Harry's Apes. I'm Harry Ainsworth and these are my monkeys." He gestured widely to his companions. "We thought that we'd come over and stay here for a while to get away from the crowds. I've got to give the boys a break. The autograph hounds have been mobbing us everywhere we've gone on this trip. We haven't had a moment's rest."

"We've got a little more luggage to carry in for you," Ted said, sidling toward the door.

But Harry was on his favorite subject. "You probably aren't aware of it living out in the sticks this way, but we're the best rock group in the country. We've played to standing room crowds every place we've gone this season. Actually, we're the hottest thing to hit America since the Beatles."

Ted and Pete looked at the door, but Harry Ainsworth did not take the hint.

"There's one more thing that I would like to ask you kids," he continued, bending low and lowering his voice. "Please don't say anything to any of the guests about who we are. We want to travel incognito, if at all possible."

They nodded mutely. *I wouldn't tell a soul that you're here,* Ted thought.

"I want to give the boys a little rest. Everywhere they go, girls are fawning over them and guys are asking for our autographs and following us around. We can't eat in privacy or relax without being stared at by people."

"We won't say anything," Pete said. "You can count on that."

Harry sauntered away importantly.

The Obnoxious Apes

"He's got quite an opinion of himself," Ted muttered.

"Not really," Pete answered sarcastically. "It's just that he assumes that we're part of his adoring public."

"He doesn't have to worry," Ted continued. "I'm not going to squeal on them. I'd like to forget I even saw them."

"If you *don't* tell, you'll break their hearts."

Ted and Pete had just deposited the last load of luggage in the singers' rooms and were about to leave when one of the guests came up to them. He seemed a little younger and friendlier than the rest.

"Hi." His smile was engaging and rather shy.

"Hello." The boys started to go out. "I think we've got everything by this time," Ted added.

"It looks it." His grin flashed. "I'm Lance Norberg."

They introduced themselves and shook hands.

"I've got a little problem," Lance said. "Maybe you fellas can help me with it."

"Sure thing," Pete responded.

"Is there any place around here where I can get some hunting arrows?"

Ted's eyes narrowed. "Hunting arrows?" he echoed. "What do you want hunting arrows for?"

"Yeah," another member of the group broke in. "Why do you want hunting arrows? You've never been able to hit anything yet, compared to *me*, anyway."

"Get off my back, will you? I just need a few good hunting arrows."

The boys eyed each other uneasily. Another archer! That made at least two in the singing group, and possibly more.

"I told you to quit fussing about those arrows," one of the others put in. "I just got a dozen new broadheads. You can have half of them if you want."

"I appreciate that, Jon, but to tell you the truth, I'd rather get my own."

"OK." Jon shrugged his indifference. "But don't say I didn't offer them to you."

"You loaned me some hunting arrows a couple days ago and they didn't do me any good."

They were still arguing good-naturedly when Ted and Pete left their room.

"Well, now, what do you think of them?" Ted asked when they were some distance away.

"As a matter of fact, they don't seem like such bad guys."

"I guess I've got to agree with you. That Harry's sort of a dope, but Lance and Jon seem to be OK."

Pete said wistfully, "I wish they weren't singing in a nightclub. I'd sort of like to hear them, wouldn't you?"

The Obnoxious Apes

"Hear them?" Ted echoed. "I hear them all the time, man. Terri doesn't even seem to know that anyone else has made any records."

* * *

In the back of the dining hall, Terri was listening with growing excitement to the other waitress.

"Did you know who's over in the lodge right now?" Sheila whispered. "You'll never guess."

"Is it someone I know?" Terri asked curiously.

"I should think so!" her friend whispered, so excited she could hardly go on. "You said that they're your favorite music group."

Terri's eyes widened and her cheeks lost their color. "The Apes?" It was more like an exclamation than a question.

"The Apes."

"You've got to be kidding."

"It's the truth. I thought I recognized Harry Ainsworth when he came into the lodge a little while ago, but I only caught a glimpse of him so I wasn't sure. I talked to Mr. Ellison just now and I was right. Harry and his Apes are going to be staying here for a few days. They might even stay until they've finished at the Eagle's Nest! Isn't that wild?"

Terry drew in her breath sharply. This wasn't true. It couldn't be. She couldn't be so fortunate as to have Harry's Apes staying at the very dude ranch where she worked. That sort of thing just didn't happen. Her heart pounded and her hands moistened with sweat.

She might even get to wait on them at mealtime! Her spirits soared! She might even be able to talk to them!

She looked up at Sheila.

"I'll make you a deal, Sheila. We don't know who's table they'll be at. Right?"

"Right."

"If I get them, you can serve them half the time. If you get them, I can serve them half the time. How about it?"

"Wonderful. That way we'll both have a chance to get to meet them."

Mrs. Ellison came by just then and both girls turned back to their work.

For Terri the rest of the afternoon dragged by endlessly. She kept looking at her watch and wishing the time away. At long last the dinner bell rang and she straightened nervously, brushing at her hair with trembling fingers.

"Do I look all right?" she asked aloud.

Mrs. Ellison stared at her questioningly. "Of course you look all right, my dear. Why shouldn't you?"

The Obnoxious Apes

Terri colored slightly, as she moved quietly to the dining room door and peeked in.

There they were! All six of them sitting at two of her tables! Her heart faltered and for an instant her knees lost their strength.

Sheila came up beside her. "See? What'd I tell you?"

"It *is* them!" Terri murmured softly, as though the very sound of her voice might be enough to break the spell and cause them to disappear.

Sheila and Terri stared at the new guests, frozen motionless by their closeness.

Mrs. Ellison came over to them. "Girls," she said quietly, "we have guests to wait on."

Mechanically, they moved out to serve them.

Jon looked up as Terri approached, his gaze surveying her slim young figure. "Hello, baby."

Lance Norberg glanced disapprovingly at him. "Lay off, Jon."

He acted as though he hadn't even heard his companion. "Well, well. The scenery just improved in here, group."

Her cheeks flamed crimson as she realized he was teasing.

"I said to lay off." Lance's voice raised. "She's just a kid."

"Since when are you your sister's keeper, Sir Lancelot?" Jon demanded.

Lance gave Jon a long, hard look. "Cool it, Jon," he said quietly.

"Who's going to make me?"

Harry Ainsworth, who acted as though he hadn't even been listening to the exchange, straightened slowly. "You heard the man, Kendall," he said sternly. "Cool it!"

Jon glared belligerently at Lance, but he settled back in his chair, mumbling to himself.

11

One Nice Ape

Terri didn't know how she ever got the orders of the group or how she managed to serve them. She didn't even know how she had been able to continue to work through the rest of the dinner. Numbly she went through the motions of serving the other guests.

A faint smile was frozen on her lips, and she did laugh when someone joked with her; but tears lurked behind her long lashes and threatened to spill down her cheeks. It had all started out so wonderfully—almost like a dream. She had been so excited a few minutes before that she could hardly contain herself. And when she saw that they were at her tables her mind almost refused to function.

Then they had to get into that stupid argument. And she had caused it. The color rushed back to her cheeks at the thought.

Lance had called her a kid! That was almost as bad as what Jon had said. Not really, she told herself quickly. She hated the look on Jon's face when he stared at her, and she certainly didn't like the way he spoke to her. He acted as though he could say anything he wanted to say to her and she wouldn't care. She had appreciated Lance's intervention. Still, he made her feel like he thought she was two or three years old and couldn't take care of herself. She figured that was why she was so upset.

When Terri finished working two hours later, Lance was waiting for her just outside the dining hall. When she opened the door and stepped out onto the porch, he straightened and started in her direction.

"Hi."

She was startled by the sound of his voice. "Oh—oh—hi."

"I didn't mean to frighten you."

"That's all right. I—" Her voice trailed away.

"I thought you would be getting off work soon, so I waited around."

"You—waited around to—to see me?" she echoed.

"I wanted to talk to you for a couple of minutes."

Terri was glad for the darkness; it hid the scarlet in her cheeks.

One Nice Ape

"I want to apologize for what happened at dinner tonight," he said. "It was inexcusable."

"It doesn't matter. It's all over now."

"But it does matter a great deal." There was an earnestness in his voice that hadn't been apparent before. "I know I'm not responsible for the things Jon does and says, but he is a member of our group. I want you to know how sorry I am that he had to act the way he did. We're not all like him. Honest."

"Thank you for coming and talking to me," Terri went on, "and I appreciate what you said to Jon tonight."

"I probably wouldn't have gotten so angry, but you remind me so much of my kid sister back in Indiana. When he started lipping off, it was almost like he was talking to her."

Terri fumbled for words. She had liked Lance from the start, but she hadn't expected him to be like a big brother to her.

"Can I walk up to the house with you?" he asked. "There are some other things I'd like to tell you."

"OK." They started in the direction of the ranch house together.

"I shouldn't be talking this way to you," Lance began, "but you do look so much like Carolyn I feel as though I have an obligation to you."

"What?"

"You'll probably meet a lot of guys like Jon before you fall in love and get married. I want to warn you. Guys like that are bad medicine, Terri. Leave them alone."

She glanced at him and smiled appreciatively. If Ted had talked to her that way her anger would have flared, but this was different.

For a long while after Terri went up to her room that night, she sat by the window, staring out into the darkness. She had never had anything quite like that happen before. Lance had seemed so sincere, so concerned about her.

He wasn't interested in dating her, and she wasn't interested in dating him. He was much too old for her. But it was just nice to know someone who cared a little.

The following morning, Jon was unusually subdued when the Apes came in to be served. He spoke to Terri, ordered breakfast, and that was all. The others spoke to Sheila and Terri with more respect than they had shown before. Both girls noticed it.

Sheila whispered, "They're real gentlemen today, aren't they?"

Terri nodded. "Especially Lance. He's still different from the others."

As soon as breakfast was over, the singers scattered. Mrs. Ellison had the cook prepare

One Nice Ape

sandwiches for them while Ted and Pete rounded up six gentle horses and saddled them.

"They said that they're going to be gone all day," Pete's mother explained.

Terri frowned. *That's strange*, she reasoned. *Awfully strange*. She had heard them talking about how tired they were. Now they were going out to ride all day. "Where are they going?"

Mrs. Ellison straightened. "Now that you mention it," she said thoughtfully, "they didn't say."

That evening after they came back Terri asked Ted if he knew where they had gone.

He shook his head. "Nope. But I did notice that two of them had their bows along."

She gasped. "You mean they're interested in archery, too?"

"Lance and Jon are. I know that much. And I'm not sure about the others." Ted pulled in a deep breath. "There's something else that bothers me about them."

"What is it?"

"I could be all wrong, but I got the idea from listening to them talk when they came in that they've been around here before."

"You must be confused."

"I know it sounds goofy, and I'm probably wrong about it, but I got the idea that they're familiar with the hills around here."

Terri ran her fingers through her hair. Ted had to be wrong about that. The group had been making personal appearances all over the country. They couldn't have spent any time in that part of the Colorado mountains—or could they? The more she thought about it the more she wondered.

The next day was like the first. The guys rode off immediately after breakfast and didn't return until almost time for dinner. Terri was so curious she asked Lance about it the first time she had a chance to see him alone.

"That's a secret," he said, laughing.

"Don't you think I can keep a secret?"

"But it wouldn't be a secret any more if I tell you." He tried to change the subject. "I just happen to have two tickets for our Thursday night's performance at the Eagle's Nest," he said. "How would you like to have them so you can attend with one of your admirers?"

Terri thought of Gary and Sam. Lance couldn't have known about them, because they both avoided her all the time now. The color rose in her cheeks. "I'm sorry, Lance," she stammered. "I don't believe I'll be going."

He stared at her quizzically, then shoved the tickets back into his pocket. "As a matter of fact, I didn't expect you to take them."

One Nice Ape

She studied his solemn face. What did he mean by that?

That night when Frank Ellison returned from town he had the fireworks for the Fourth of July display.

"They finally came," he told Ted and Pete. "I was beginning to think that we were going to have to call off the display this year."

"Now we can go out and scare Prince Atlas so bad he'll never trust man again as long as he lives," Pete said.

"After you ride fence tomorrow morning," his father reminded him.

"Oh, Dad!" he groaned aloud.

"The work here at the ranch has to go on too, you know. We have our stock to take care of first."

"But you know what might happen to him."

Mr. Ellison nodded. "Next time, perhaps you'll be a little more careful about what you do. Then things like this won't happen."

Ted told Terri about it when he saw her later that evening.

"And I'm afraid Harry's Apes are a bunch of illegal archers trying to get a shot at some animal like Prince," he concluded.

"It could be," she said thoughtfully. "They do act like hunters, the way they leave in the morning and stay all day."

Ted shook his head. "They're up to something," he said firmly, "and I don't know what."

Terri looked in the direction of Bald Mountain. "I'd just *die* if something would happen to Prince," she said softly.

An idea suddenly hit Ted. "You know, *you* could help us find out if they're after Prince Atlas. And that would let us know what to expect."

"How could *I* find out anything like that?" she asked.

"You're friendly enough with that Lance Norberg guy. Get him talking and pry the information out of him."

"Do you think I could?"

"You'd have a lot better chance of doing it than any of the rest of us. That's for sure."

She thought about Lance. She had the next day off, and she just might be able to convince him that he ought to take her riding. That would be the best way. In fact, it was the only way she could think of that would give her enough time with him alone to find out anything at all.

She sighed deeply. She didn't even know for sure if she could get him to let her join him. He was nice, but there were times when he wasn't too friendly.

She went back over to the dining hall and to the main lodge to find Lance and talk to him, but he was nowhere around. She almost decided that he

One Nice Ape

had left the ranch for the evening when she caught a glimpse of him walking from the station wagon toward his room.

"Oh, Lance!" Her youthful voice sang out musically.

He stopped and turned. "It's you, Terri. I wondered who was calling me."

"I've been looking all over for you."

"Oh?" His voice was controlled. "And what is the reason that I'm so honored?"

"I have the day off tomorrow," she announced.

He laughed genially. "Is that supposed to be significant?"

"I'd like to go riding with you tomorrow," she said.

"Go riding with me? Aren't you a little young for a twenty-four-year-old?"

She felt embarrassed, but she had to go on. "You'd take your sister on a picnic with you if she was here, wouldn't you?"

"I suppose so."

"Then, that's the way I'd like to go. Not as a—a girlfriend, but as your sister."

Lance thought about that.

"You don't think the Ellisons and your brother would get the wrong idea if we go somewhere together, do you? I wouldn't want them to think I was dating you."

"I'll tell them," she blurted. "I'll make them understand that there's nothing between us at all, that we're just friends."

Reluctantly, Lance agreed. "You've got to promise to do as I tell you and stay out of the way, if I take you with me. I can't have you ruining things."

"Like what?" she asked pointedly.

He glared at her. "Like—like *things!*" he repeated. "I'll have to know that you're not going to give me any problems. This is serious business as far as we're concerned."

Curiosity filled her head with questions, but she forced herself to say, "I promise."

"Then you've got yourself a deal!" He grinned self-consciously. "I'm glad you're going with me tomorrow, Terri. I get more lonesome for that sister of mine than anyone else in the family. You'll help me keep from getting homesick."

"I'll be ready when you are in the morning," she told him. An instant later she had said good-bye and was hurrying away.

12

An Unexpected Foe

Terri didn't know what time Lance planned to leave the following morning, but she got up at the usual time, had breakfast, and was waiting for him. Shortly after eight o'clock he came down to the barn to get his saddle horse.

"I thought maybe you'd change your mind," he said.

"I should say not. I've been looking forward to this."

"OK. Let's get saddled up and on our way. We've got a lot of ground to cover." As they started into the barn he paused, staring at Ted and Pete who were riding toward the far end of the pasture. "Where are they going so early?"

"They've got some fence-tending to do," she explained.

"So early in the morning?"

"They want to get back as quick as they can.

They've got something else to do as soon as possible."

Lance went into the barn and picked up his saddle. "Ted and Pete have been acting awfully strange toward me lately. What's the deal?"

She turned away quickly so he couldn't read the consternation in her eyes. "You'll have to ask them," she said coyly.

"They're awful curious all of a sudden." He paused significantly. "And especially that brother of yours. He acts like he expects us to report to him every time we make a move."

Terri frowned. She didn't like having anyone find fault with Ted; not even Lance. She couldn't blame Ted for being suspicious after all that had happened to Prince Atlas and the danger the little elk was in. She was suspicious too.

"I'm sure that's an exaggeration," she said icily.

"You don't have to get so shook up about it. I was just telling you how I felt. I didn't mean anything personal by it."

"That's nice."

They saddled their horses without further conversation, led them outside to water, and put the bridles on.

Terri wasn't even sure that she wanted to go riding with Lance after the way he had been talking that morning. She was afraid she wouldn't enjoy it.

An Unexpected Foe

"Well, I guess we're ready to go." Lance put a foot in the stirrup and swung onto his rangy mount.

"Which way are we going to ride?" she asked.

He grinned crookedly. "Suppose we wait and find out, OK?"

"It would be nice to know so I could tell Mrs. Ellison. She always likes to know where we're going and what time we'll be back."

Lance's gaze met hers. "You can tell her that we're going up on the ridge." He gestured widely with his hand. "And we'll be back some time in the middle of the afternoon."

After stopping at the house to relay that information to the rancher's wife, they left the ranch yard and headed in the direction of the far ridge.

"It's nice having you along, Terri," the singer said. "It makes me think of the times Carolyn and I used to go horseback riding. As a matter of fact, we still go when I have time enough to do it."

They rode on for several minutes in comparative silence.

"Tell me," she said, coming back to the subject once more, "where are we going?"

"You're as curious as that brother of yours."

She drew herself erect. "If you don't want me to go, perhaps I'd better turn around and go back to the M-Bar-H."

"That would be a waste after talking me into bringing you with me."

She felt the color rise in her cheeks. "I thought it would be fun, but if we're going to quarrel all the time—"

He laughed. "You are just like Carolyn. You've got a lot of spunk."

At the fork in the trail, Lance followed the one that Terri and Gary had taken ten days before.

"Do we have to go this way?" she asked uneasily.

"Mind telling me what's wrong with going this way?"

She squirmed uncomfortably. "Nothing, I guess."

"Then quit complaining. This happens to be the way that I want to go."

"But—"

He urged his mount ahead, even faster than before. At the cliff he hesitated only long enough to glance back at Terri. "Can you ride over this stretch of the trail?" he asked.

She paused. "And what if I can't?"

"Then I guess it would be best if you turned around and went back."

She stiffened. She didn't want to cross the sheer cliff on the narrow trail, but she had no choice. She wouldn't find out what Lance, and maybe the others, were up to unless she did.

"I've done it before," she said.

An Unexpected Foe

"So have I."

Terri noticed the tone in his voice. What did he mean by that? She wished she had the courage to ask him.

Crossing the cliff hadn't been as difficult for Terri this time as it had been when she went over it with Gary. Lance's calm assurance was encouraging.

Once over the cliff Lance took another left turn at a fork in the trail, and Terri relaxed. They had left the trail that led to the sheepherder's cabin. Ted must have been wrong. At least Lance didn't seem to be interested in the elk.

After a quarter of a mile on the new trail that led even higher up the ridge, Lance stopped suddenly. "Wait here, Terri. I'll be back in a jiff."

"Where are you going?" She acted as if she was going to dismount and go with him.

"Just wait here. I'll be right back," he commanded.

"But where are you going?"

His patience wore through. "Up to an abandoned cabin to get something," he retorted irritably. "I'll be back in a few minutes."

He started up a steep footpath, but turned and came back.

"Terri, there's one thing I've got to ask you. Can you keep a secret?"

"I think so."

"Will you promise me that you'll keep this a secret?" he asked.

"Of course I will."

"And you won't tell anybody?"

"I won't tell anybody."

"No matter what?"

Now her anger flashed. "If you don't trust me, perhaps I had better turn around and go back. I've already given you my word, haven't I?"

"OK." He relaxed and grinned. "I just have to be sure, that's all."

When he came back several minutes later he was carrying a bow and a quiver full of arrows. She stared at them suspiciously.

"And what are you doing with a bow out here?" she demanded.

"I loaned it to a guy a few days ago and he left it out here. Can you imagine that?"

"It seems like a strange place to leave a bow," she told him.

"That's what I said when he came back and told me what he'd done." Lance shrugged. "I figured that as long as we're in this area I'd stop and pick up my gear before somebody steals it."

She did not answer him. The arrows in his quiver were vaguely familiar.

They rode on for several minutes without

An Unexpected Foe

speaking to each other. At last Lance spoke, thoughtfully.

"Are you sure you wouldn't like to have a couple of tickets to one of our performances at the Eagle's Nest?" he asked.

"No, thank you." She couldn't look in his direction.

"I offered that brother of yours a couple, but he turned me down too. Have you got the same reason?"

She felt her uneasiness growing. "What reason did Ted give for not going?" As if she didn't know! Now Lance was probably thinking of her as a religious fanatic, the same as her brother.

He reined to a stop and turned around in the saddle to face her. "Are you sure that you don't know?"

She opened her mouth to deny it but stopped herself. She couldn't lie about it. "He told you he didn't want to go because he's a Christian and felt that it's best for him to stay away from places like the Eagle's Nest."

Lance nodded.

Terri squirmed. She knew that he was waiting for her to continue.

"That's the same reason I don't want to go," she stammered. Now he would laugh at her, and before the day was out all the guys in the singing group would know what kind of a nut she was. She could hear them saying that Terri Walker had "freaked out" over religion.

But Lance didn't laugh. Instead a strange look came into his eyes.

"My folks and my little sister, Carolyn, believe the same as you and your brother." He managed an embarrassed laugh. "They don't even like the idea of my playing in an outfit like the Apes. They keep writing that they're praying for me."

His openness gave Terri courage. "Maybe you ought to consider the claims the Lord Jesus Christ has on your life too, Lance. You know, He died on the cross for you the same as He did for me and your parents and your sister, Carolyn."

For an instant it seemed that he was hesitating, touched by what she had told him. Then a hardness tightened the corners of his mouth. He shrugged his shoulders as if to shrug off what she had said.

"Can't do it, Terri. I've got my career to think about. Everything I've dreamed and worked for would go down the drain if I believed in Christ."

That seemed to resolve the matter. He quit talking and urged his horse on with a sharp kick in the flanks.

Terri followed him mutely. Numbness took hold of her. Lance seemed to be so close to making a

An Unexpected Foe

decision for Christ. If only she could say the right thing! If only she could quote the right Bible verses!

He seemed to be more nervous than ever now. He squirmed in the saddle and kept looking at his watch.

"Are you expecting to meet someone?" she asked after a time.

"Oh, no. It's not that at all. I've just been thinking that I'd like to ride up to the top of the ridge," he told her lamely. "And if I do, I'm sure it'll be close to dark before I get back."

She eyed him curiously. He didn't sound sincere. He sounded as if he were making excuses, that he actually was trying to get rid of her.

"I don't think I can stay that long. Mrs. Ellison and Ted would be frantic by the time I got back." She paused. "Would you like to have me go back alone?"

"I hate to have you do that." Reluctance crept into his voice. "I can come up here another time."

"It won't bother me at all," she said. "I can easily make it back to the ranch. So why don't you go on up to wherever you would like to go?"

"I shouldn't leave you to ride home alone, Terri."

"I don't know why not. This is the second summer we've spent here. I've learned how to take care of myself."

"Well," he replied, obviously relieved, "if you're

sure that you can manage, I would like to go on up the ridge."

"Would you like to have me take the bow and your arrows home for you?"

Looking at him, she thought his cheeks darkened slightly. "Oh, no," he said quickly. "I might decide to do a little target practice along the way."

Terri said good-bye and left him. She really didn't think about what he had said regarding the bow until she was a quarter of a mile away. He was upset by her suggestion that she take the bow home for him, and the reason he gave for not doing it wasn't logical. The ride to the top of the ridge was a long one. Even though he had several hours of daylight, he would have to keep riding if he wanted to make it up there and back before darkness closed out the trail.

Those arrows! She suddenly remembered where she had seen one like them! The broken arrow that Ted and Pete had found at the old sheepherder's place!

In an instant the pieces to the puzzle fell into place. Lance had indeed been in that area before. And he had shot an arrow at Prince Atlas. The bow and arrows were his, all right, but no one else had left them up at the old cabin. *He* must have stashed them away. Now he wanted to get rid of her so he could go after Prince without being seen!

An Unexpected Foe

Terri pulled in a deep breath.

She didn't know why Lance had brought her along in the first place, if he had been intent on going out after Prince Atlas that day. Or, why he had decided to go hunting so early. She had been questioning Mr. Ellison and some of the older wranglers at the M-Bar-H after she and Gary had found Prince and Gary almost shot him. They all said that at this particular time of year it was better to hunt at dusk. That was the time the elk usually came into the clearings to feed.

Maybe Lance had decided to go hunting after he and Terri left the ranch, or maybe he had figured that she would be able to help him find the elk and that she wouldn't tell on him. If that was the reason, then why did he change his mind?

It could be that Lance had figured all along on sending her home before he started hunting. He may have wanted to get rid of her so he could sneak up to the sheepherder's clearing and secret himself before twilight brought the elk out to feed. That made more sense than his trying to stalk Prince during the day, when the chances were that he wasn't moving around much.

But those things didn't matter now. There would be plenty of time to ask questions and expect answers later, after she had made sure that Prince Atlas was safe.

For an instant she paused, uncertain as to what to do. She could follow Lance and try to ruin his shot by chasing Prince away, but that would make Lance terribly mad. She wouldn't dare risk that. Besides, he might discover her before he reached the clearing, or he could manage to lose her in the forest. Also, he would undoubtedly stay on the mountain until after dark. That would mean that she would not get home until far later than what she had told Mrs. Ellison.

No, it would be better for her to dash back to the ranch and tell Mr. Ellison and the boys what had happened. If they came in the jeep, they would still be able to reach the clearing an hour before sundown. That would be the safest way to handle it.

She urged her pony into a fast lope with a kick of her heels and an unspoken prayer. Everything depended on her getting back to the ranch as quickly as possible.

13

Safe at Last

Terri rode along at a steady, distance-eating lope until she reached the narrow stretch of trail that skirted the sheer granite cliff. There she reined up to let the pony pick his way across the treacherous ledge.

Then it happened!

An ominous rattle broke the silence. A rattlesnake! The horse squealed in terror and reared, twisting himself backward from the snake. Terri was thrown from the saddle, and the reins jerked from her grip as the horse bolted. He charged away in panic, leaving Terri lying stunned on the ground.

It was almost a minute before she was able to move. She groaned weakly and rolled over onto her side. The fall had knocked the wind from her lungs, and she gasped and choked as she struggled to breathe.

Slowly her breath came back to her, and she was

able to get to her feet. Neither the snake nor her saddle horse was in sight. As she stood there, the seriousness of her situation became apparent to her. She would never be able to get down to the ranch in time to get help to save Prince Atlas now!

She started forward uncertainly, heading back toward the cliff without thinking. Once there she stopped, the numbness inside of her increasing. She had wasted another few minutes by not heading down toward the trail.

And then she saw them! Two horsemen were heading leisurely up the path below her. Her heart leaped! The horses and the riders looked familiar. Could it be—?

Yes! There on the trail below rode Ted and Pete! If she could only attract their attention!

Ted and Pete were still quite a long way from the base of the cliff, but she was sure that they would be able to hear her.

"Ted!" she shouted as loudly as she could, cupping her hands to her mouth. "Ted! Pete!"

But they rode along without even looking up.

She called to them again and again, but they did not even glance in her direction. In a short time they would pass the bend in the trail that lay closest to the cliff and would be heading almost directly away from it. She had to get down to where she could be heard. She *had* to make them hear!

An Unexpected Foe   119

"O God, help me!" she prayed.

If she could just find a place where she could climb down the cliff quickly, she might be able to cross the little stream and get to the trail before they passed.

She hurried along the steep cliff until she came to a place where she thought she might be able to get down. It was so steep it took her breath away. But grimly she started downward. Her breathing was short and quick and her head whirled, but she could not stop. She had to get down and get Ted and Pete to help her while there was still time!

It was not too bad at first. The cliff was steep, but there were plenty of rocks and clumps of brush for handholds. She was going faster than she had thought she could, and for the moment she began to breathe more easily.

Terri made her way down twenty-five feet, and then fifty, and then seventy-five feet. The going got a little harder, but by this time she was gaining confidence.

"O God," she prayed again, "thank You for helping me!"

Again she stopped for breath, taking a quick glance back in the direction Ted and Pete were coming. They were not hurrying. She was thankful for that. She could see them plainly now. They were looking at one another, talking; and the horses were picking their own gait. But she had to keep moving. She couldn't even stop for rest. In a few short minutes they would be rounding the bend and going away from the cliff.

She had been inching downward steadily for some minutes, but now it seemed that all at once the cliff was almost perpendicular. There was scarcely any place to put her feet, and the handholds were less secure. Every now and then she came to a few feet of loose shale.

Terri thought of calling out to them, but she didn't dare take the time or the energy. They were still some distance away, and probably wouldn't hear her. She had to keep going just as fast as she could.

She didn't notice that the loose shale grew heavier and more treacherous, or that the few scraggly weeds and bushes that fought against the stone clung precariously in place by slim roots.

She inched forward. She was well out on the shale when she realized how insecure her footing was. Fear gripped her. Her foot began to slip, only a little at first. She tightened her body and reached for a small tree. Her weight pulled against it. The roots gave way!

"O God, help me!"

Terri did not know how far she slipped. It seemed to be at least a hundred feet but was proba-

An Unexpected Foe

bly closer to ten. When she finally succeeded in clutching something strong enough to hold her, her feet were dangling out into open space.

For a long, agonizing moment she clung there without trying to move. Breath rasped out of her lungs, searing them like fire.

Terri tried desperately to pull herself up, but she could not. The strength drained rapidly from her arms and fingers.

"Ted!" she cried in desperation. "Help!"

Her words echoed and reechoed, unanswered, across the valley.

How long she clung to the cliff she did not know. Her arms ached and her fingers throbbed with pain as she dug into the rocks.

She prayed silently for help.

She could not hang on much longer. Her head was whirling; and her fingers, moist with sweat, throbbed until she knew she could not dig them into the rock any longer.

"Ted!" she shouted.

But it was no use! They could not hear her! She sobbed in agony. No one could hear her!

* * *

On the trail where Terri had been a few moments before, Lance was riding in the direction of the cliff, his very being in a turmoil. He didn't know why talking with Terri had upset him so much that he gave up the hunt. He certainly hadn't planned it that way.

He supposed it was because of what she had said about Christ and living for Him. It was no wonder she reminded him of his sister. They both talked the same way.

He had decided to ride back to the ranch and make up some sort of a story to satisfy Jon and the others—some reason for not tracking down the little elk and getting another shot at him.

Lance slumped in the saddle. It had been years since he had thought about his own need of the Lord Jesus Christ. When he quit college and joined the Apes, it hadn't even bothered his conscience. When his folks and Carolyn heard about it and wrote that they were heartbroken, he read the letter to the rest of the guys so they could all have a good laugh.

Now all the past descended upon him with a rush. He had never felt so wicked in his life.

At that instant Lance heard a weak cry. He reined in suddenly and strained to catch the sound again. There it was, a thin cry of desperation.

A chill surged through him! Terri! He recognized her voice!

Lance stopped at the edge of the cliff, swung to

An Unexpected Foe

the ground, and ran forward. "Hang on, Terri! I'm coming!"

She heard his voice sounding faint and far away. Her heart leaped.

"Hang on!"

She didn't know whether she could or not. It seemed as though all the strength had drained from her body and that she couldn't hang on for another moment.

Lance moved swiftly, expertly down the steep cliff. He had done a lot of climbing on college field trips, and the sheer wall didn't bother him at all. He moved downward effortlessly and with surprising speed.

It seemed to Terri that it took hours for him to reach her. One by one, her fingers began to slip. She pressed them against the sharp rocks so desperately that they began to bleed.

Lance made his way past her and put his hand under her foot. "Now, take it easy," he said, panting, "and do exactly as I tell you!"

"I can't hold on any longer!"

"You've *got* to!" His voice was stern. "Now let your feet down to the ledge."

"But if I move I—I'll fall!"

"I'll hold your weight. Just hang on as much as you can and work your hands down over the rock.

I've got good footing so you won't need to be afraid that you're going to fall."

"I'll try," she whispered.

It scarcely seemed possible that he could hold her, balanced as he was on the thin ledge. But she did exactly as he had directed her, and in a moment she had her feet safely on the rocky ledge. She clung to her handholds in desperation, unable to move for a moment.

"I—I thought sure I was going to fall!" She could feel herself trembling all over.

"Follow me," he told her when she had her breath. "The worst is over now. It's not going to be bad from here on down. I'll help you if you get into trouble."

"I don't think I can make it."

"You've got to."

He began to move along the ledge slowly, working his way downward. Although Terri did not think she could take another step, she managed to follow him. And as she did so, it seemed that her strength began to come back. Finally they were on the ground.

Gasping with relief and exhaustion, Terri dropped to the rocky ground at the base of the cliff. Ted and Pete stared numbly at her and Lance.

"We heard you," her twin brother murmured, "but we couldn't have gotten to you in time!"

An Unexpected Foe

"That's right," Pete put in. "We were about frantic trying to figure out what to do until we saw Lance coming toward you."

"We can thank God you heard Terri, Lance," Ted said.

There was a long, painful silence.

* * *

Back at the ranch the next morning Ted turned to his sister. "We took care of Prince Atlas," he said. "We won't have to worry about him being so tame that he'll let a hunter walk up within range anymore."

Pete laughed. "You can say that again. We tied some of those big firecrackers to arrows and Lance shot them in Prince's direction. You should've seen him take off!"

Terri nodded. "I tried to thank him for it before he left, but he wouldn't let me."

Pete asked, "Why did he quit the Apes and take off for home the way he did? That was something I couldn't understand."

"I asked him about it," she continued. "He said that he'd finally seen that he had to commit his life to Christ if he wanted to be happy."

"He did?" Ted's eyes widened. "I didn't know he was even interested."

"He said he was going home and talk to the

pastor of the church his family attends. He said he has a lot of things to get straightened out."

"That's wonderful!" Ted exclaimed.

"Dad and Mother were surprised when Harry and his Apes moved out the first thing this morning," Pete told the Walker twins. "Harry said he had to get his gang out of here. He was afraid he'd lose the rest of them if he didn't."

Moody Press, a ministry of the Moody Bible Institute, is designed for education, evangelization and edification. If we may assist you in knowing more about Christ and the Christian life, please write us without obligation to: Moody Press, c/o MLM, Chicago, Illinois 60610.